T5-AWI-159

My Life With Dogs

By
Gayle Bunney

© 1999 by Lone Pine Publishing
First printed in 1999   10 9 8 7 6 5 4 3 2 1
Printed in Canada

All rights reserved. No part of this work covered by the copyrights hereon may be reproduced or used in any form or by any means—graphic, electronic or mechanical—without the prior written permission of the publisher, except for reviewers, who may quote brief passages. Any request for photocopying, recording, taping or storage on information retrieval systems of any part of this work shall be directed in writing to the publisher.

The Publisher: Lone Pine Publishing

10145 – 81 Ave.   1901 Raymond Ave. SW, Suite C
Edmonton, AB T6E 1W9   Renton, WA 98055
Canada   USA

Website: http://www.lonepinepublishing.com

Canadian Cataloguing in Publication Data

Bunney, Gayle, 1954–
    My Life With Dogs

    ISBN 1–55105–152–4

    1. Dogs—Anecdotes. I. Title.
SF426.2.B86 1999   636.7   C99–911022–5

Editorial Director: Nancy Foulds
Project Editor: Erin McCloskey
Production Manager: Jody Reekie
Book Design: Michelle Bynoe
Layout & Production: Michelle Bynoe
Illustrations: Linda Dunn
Book Cover Design: Rob Weidemann
Cover Illustration: Gary Ross

We acknowledge the financial support of the Government of Canada through the Book Publishing Industry Development Program (BPIDP) for our publishing activities.

PC: P6

Canadä

I WISH TO THANK

For all the help they give me, I wish to thank, my friends, especially Margo Morton. Also, Dr. Neil Cory and his wonderful family.

But most of all, these dogs who give me everything. For I was nothing, until they showed me true love and happiness. Thank you my friends, both human and four-legged.

CONTENTS

PREFACE

Since I was a small child, I have known of the special bond I have with all animals. To the old antelope, who made the journey back early each year, by herself, no herd, to have her calf next to my dad's Hereford cattle, I was nothing more than a sprite when I reached out and touched her on the shoulder.

With the big, old badger Dad, as both farmer and cattleman, had to dispose of if at all possible, I laid quietly on the ground in front of his den and tried to tell him, it was best to leave so he wouldn't get hurt. How he finally, with bared fangs and mad at the whole world, came out of his burrow, with narrowed eyes, to listen to me. Inches from my young face, he laid there and seemed to think about it. Did my talk do any good? I don't know. I just know that Dad never did come home for supper and say that he had disposed of the badger.

My brothers tried to make pets out of prairie jack rabbits, orphaned by the machines that planted the spring crops. How I felt their wish for freedom, never to be truly tamed by man.

From the family dogs, to the wild grey dove with the injured wing, I was at home with God's creatures. Let me tell you about my life with my dogs, who depend upon me daily not only for food and water, but also for a kind hand and a bit of love.

Come walk beside me and my four-legged friends as you read of our happiness and sorrows; of the good times and the bad; of birth and death. Come, read and remember.

LIKE MOTHER, LIKE DAUGHTER

Where do I get my love for animals? Perhaps my need to live with them and be a total part of them comes from my sweet mother.

My mother's favourite horse, Flip, was so badly abused that she trusted no one—nobody except my mother, who led her gently by a handful of mane hair so as to not frighten her by touching her head. The bay mare, Beauty, trusted Mom enough to go right into the house with her. The colt, Blazer, who Mom raised by hand when his own mother died of a heart attack giving birth, was fed milk from a bowl, clutched in Mom's young hands. Until that horse was four years of age, he expected Mom to feed him his water from that very bowl. Her pet sheep, Tilly, always slept under her bedroom window to be close to her. One day, when the farm dogs scared Tilly half to death, she plunged right through the screen door to get to Mom. She knew who loved and protected her.

When Mom's older brother, Raymond, would take after her teasingly, she simply had to make a mad dash out to the big, mean, old goose. There in the barnyard, she would stand with her hand resting on top of the male gander's head. At only four or five years old, she was barely taller than the goose. Snaking his head in rage, hissing like a demon, he prevented Uncle Raymond from getting anywhere near Mom.

The dogs were especially fond of Mom's love and attention. In return, Brownie, the Collie, would not let Granddad even think about giving Mom a spanking for some misdeed. Brownie would stand between Granddad and Mom with his teeth bared and hackles raised to protect her. Buster, a small Collie-type, loved to swing with her. There Mom would be, swinging higher and higher with Buster's jaws latched onto her ankle, swinging right along with her. He held her so gently that not a tooth mark could ever be found on her skin. Heck, my Mom gave and received more love from the animals than most dogs have fleas.

When my day's work is finally done, and I can sit down, I am at peace with the world. My dogs gather at my feet. Some find the space to squeeze amongst others on my lap. Trixie will be draped around my neck, resting mostly on the cushioned chair back. As I talk to them, each one in turn responds to his or her name by wiggling just a bit closer to me, happy that I haven't forgotten them. Half-grown pups must wait more to the outside of the ring of dogs surrounding me. They know they are not forgotten though. They know they will get a hug and a kiss on their cool noses, before I turn in for the night. I am blessed.

YOU GOTTA LUV THEM

You just have to love these four-legged rascals who, since ancient times, have shared our homes. To me they are not just dogs, but intelligent, warm, loving creations who often make better friends than the two-legged kind. Of course, they do pull some strange stunts that humans don't normally pull. Take Pebbles, my Dalmatian, for instance. She's a super mother to her young pups, but can go overboard occasionally when concerned about their welfare. Deciding the laundry room wasn't cozy enough for her three-week-old babies, she carefully moved them one at a time to a new location. Imagine the look on my face in the morning, when with half-closed eyes I made my way to the bathroom, took a seat, yawned and happened to look in the bathtub at the little black spots all over the bottom of it.

I wasn't about to go for weeks without a bath, until they were weaned and old enough to sell, so I hauled them back to the laundry room. Pebbles simply hauled them back to the tub.

This went on for most of the day until I, not Pebbles, gave up. I compromised, setting them out on the floor while I used the tub, dried the tub each time and helped Pebbles put them back in. She was quite disgusted with her wee ones when they soon became too big for such a small space and demanded to be allowed to live elsewhere.

In the wild, canines introduce their young to solid food, by first eating the food themselves, letting it partially digest and then regurgitating it for them. Well, Pebbles figured what was good enough for her ancient ancestors was good enough for her. Her puppies might have liked it, but personally I found watching it a little hard to stomach.

Now, as far as I have been able to figure, a dog is always starving to death. All my dogs are borderline overweight and always have dry food in front of them and soft food should they require it, yet the second I sit down to munch on lunch, every one of them acts as if they haven't been fed for a week of Sundays. Deciding that I too am borderline overweight, I drag out the celery, carrots, lettuce and bean sprouts out of the fridge. While standing at the kitchen counter, slicing and peeling, I sometimes accidentally drop a carrot stick or a lettuce leaf on the floor. One or two of the dogs might mosey over and sniff at it, but eat it, never. But if I sit down at the table with this rabbit food piled on my plate, quicker than you can say "Bugs Bunny," I am surrounded by starving dogs. Tongues hanging out, eyes pleading, they silently beg for just a tiny morsel of food to keep them alive. If I drop a carrot stick it is snapped up in someone's drooling jaws. A sprinkling of bean sprouts hitting the floor causes a riot of animals fighting to see who can swallow the most, the fastest. I guess you can see why I am tempted to hide in the hall closet when eating steak or hamburger.

Puppies love to chew, in fact they have to chew in order to have strong, clean, healthy teeth. So, of course, I supply them

9

with safe and durable chew toys. Rope toys, stuffed toys, rawhide bones, you name it, my puppies have it. So why do they insist that my shoes and clothes make better chew toys than the roomful they already have? Little pups aren't too bad really, as long as you rescue your valuables as quickly as possible. Older pups, just passing through their teenage years, are the worst. I'm convinced that their teeth, regardless of the size of dog, are in that mouth to cause total destruction and nothing else. Between the ages of six months and one year, Bailey, one of my prettiest Toy Poodles, managed to chew her way through everything in my house. People come to visit and wonder why my toilet paper does not hang on the wall, but instead sits up on the back of the toilet tank. Bailey taught me to do that after she went through four new rolls in one day alone. People wonder why my shoes and boots sit away up on top of my microwave stand in the kitchen. Bailey taught me to do that too. People wonder why the door to my bedroom is always closed. Well, my bedroom has things like socks, shorts and slippers in it and Bailey taught me to keep my door firmly closed. I keep thinking something is wrong with my relationship with dogs. Aren't I supposed to be teaching them things instead of them teaching me things?

Even my Cockapoo, Racey, has managed to teach me things. Her favourite puppy habit, which thank heavens she has finally outgrown, taught me to mop up the kitchen floor half a dozen times a day. I have a couple of water dishes on the floor and, like a good dog owner, I try to keep them full of fresh, clean water at all times. Racey's favourite game was to get the water out of these dishes as quickly as possible, as often as possible. They are non-spillable dishes that can't be flipped over. Racey would simply get both her furry front paws into the dish and paw like she was digging a hole to China. Presto, water everywhere and one happy, soaking wet Cockapoo pup. I learnt to be pretty handy with that old mop.

My sweet dog, Annie, taught me to have minor heart attacks every time she grabbed a horse's tail in her teeth and swung joyfully back and forth on it.

Polly taught me to get used to finding dead birds and small animals in the house. Her pride and joy was probably the dead garter snake (I think it was a snake, but in really bad shape) she brought home and refused to give up when I wanted to throw it in the garbage. You can imagine me inviting company into my house and saying, "just let me get that dead duck off that chair before you sit down and yes, that really is a two-foot dead snake hanging out of that dog's mouth." "Pardon me, what is that lump of decaying fur over there in the corner?" my guests would ask. "Oh nothing really, probably it was a gopher or a mouse or something at one time." I sure do love that Polly dog of mine.

RESCUED DOGS

I have always had a soft spot for the unwanted, unloved and uncared-for creatures. Horses, cats, dogs and even a couple of cows have ended up at my place in need of food and love. My heart goes out to dogs perhaps the most of all. Their trusting nature, their desire to please even the most cruel of masters and the way their tails always manage to wag regardless of starvation or injury, these are some of the reasons my eyes mist over at the sight of a dog in need.

I remember the scraggly mongrel who died in my arms after I found it wandering aimlessly, far out in the bush, miles from civilization. The only way he could have got there was by the hands of an uncaring master who dropped him off, leaving him to the mercy of starvation and wild animals. Although I took him home and tried to nurse him back to health, he was too far gone to even try to eat. An advanced case of a canine disease made his passing all the more painful.

I am always appalled at the way some people's minds work. They decide they don't want the dog anymore so they take him out to the country and throw him out of the car. They perhaps justify doing so believing that some farmer will give him a home.

Somebody, who likely knew my reputation for taking in strays, left five, tiny, brown, mixed-breed pups, no more than four weeks old in a cardboard box in my driveway approach. Following the neighbourhood school bus home from town, it continued past my place, while I slowed to turn into my yard. The school bus's tires had passed over what appeared at first glance to be a pile of horse manure on the road. That pile of horse manure was those five babies who had tipped the box over and ended up curled in the middle of the road. Not one of them survived.

I had answered an ad in the city paper stating an adult

female American Cocker Spaniel was for sale. The second I saw her I said to myself, no way do I want this dog. She was a rack of bones with dead hair clinging to them. Bending down I stroked her head and caught a whiff of what was to turn out to be the worst, almost untreatable, ear infection I've ever encountered. I just couldn't afford to pay out good money for this animal. While I was telling myself this, I made the mistake of looking into those big, soulful Cocker Spaniel eyes. She stared up at me, silently pleading with me for just one more gentle pat on the head. Then she cinched it by wagging her stubby tail at me. I paid the owner and headed home with my new dog. The cab of the truck was soon full of the stink of those ears. Within a few days, every one of my canine friends was busy scratching the fleas she brought home with her. To better treat her large population of creepy crawlies, I shaved her down to the skin. As the filthy matted hair fell away from her, I discovered not only fleas but also lice. You can well imagine what it ended up costing me, to do a complete flea and lice treatment on all my dogs, my house and kennels. As for her ears, she turned out to be almost deaf from the infection at less than three years of age. Although I have faithfully continued to treat them with every product on the market, I still can't get her ears cleared up. All I can do is keep trying. She is a wonderful dog now though, especially since gaining weight and growing a new coat of soft, clean hair. She's definitely a keeper.

I rescued a dog from a city pound one time who went on to lead the life of Reilly. He was a stray lassie dog who had been picked up by a dogcatcher. He was simply gorgeous to look at. His personality was tops. But he had a problem, which meant he was not for adoption. He had a severe cold, bordering on pneumonia. So it had been decided to just put him to sleep. A volunteer worker at the pound phoned me and told me about this friendly, golden clown of a dog, who would be put down the next day, unless she could convince the pound that I would take the dog and have it treated properly by a veterinarian. So I came home with another stray, unwanted dog. It took some time to clear up his medical problem and, unable to keep him myself, I set out to find him a new home.

My close friend, Bill, had just brought home his new bride, June, from England. Now, the English are rather fond of their dogs and, knowing June was lonesome out on the farm in this new country, I showed up with the dog and a giant bag of dog food and proceeded to tell her that this was my welcome to Canada gift. I often visited June and her faithful companion— the dog that is, not Bill—and what a pair they were. She spoiled him to no end, even blowing his nose for him, with a clean hanky if he so much as snuffled. Another dog, another happy ending.

I once had to rescue the same dog twice. I heard from another kennel owner that still another kennel owner, who was not good to her dogs, in any way, shape or form, was going to have a family member shoot two of her old Poodles because she no longer wanted to use them for breeding. They were just two old dogs who had lived the best years of their lives in unheated, outdoor kennels, starved for a kind word or a lap to lie on. She figured no one would want the old dogs so she wasn't even bothering to try and give them away. So I showed up and offered to take them. She charged me fifty dollars for each of them even though she confirmed she was disposing of them anyway. So home I go with the two smelly, untrimmed Poodles.

Dagwood, the chocolate-coloured one, was some homely. She had purchased him at about a year-old in the States, where his first owners had treated him fair and house trained him. Even after living in an old barn outside all that time, he still remembered his house training and I soon found a caring and loving home for him. Odie, the smaller one, had an infected eye so I wanted to clear that up before finding him a home.

Now, he had lived all his life in a pen, approximately four feet square, and knew nothing about being house trained. He also did not know how to walk or run in a straight line like a normal dog. All the poor thing knew how to do was spin around and around as if he was still confined to that dreadfully small space. There he would be in the middle of my kitchen floor, frantically spinning around in his tight circle, but oh so happy to be with the other dogs and me. When I took him outside, he would start out following me, then forget he was free at last, and around in his circle he would go again. He was so frightened by the electric clippers that I put off giving him a hair cut, just using the scissors to remove the worst of the mattes.

I hadn't had him long when his life took another wrong turn. I had the whole pack out on the lawn exercising when I heard the phone ringing. I dashed into the house to find it was a long distance phone call. I barely started talking when I heard a vehicle slow down and stop out on the road. A few seconds later, I heard a door slam and the vehicle accelerated away at top speed. By the time I could get back outside, I was short one dog. Odie had been stolen in broad daylight from my yard. Even though I advertised in the local papers and over the radio, offering a good-sized reward for the return of the dog, nothing came of it. I feared since Odie was scruffy, not completely house trained and with an infected eye, that whoever stole him would just get rid of him.

It was around a year later when Odie came back into my life. The local dog catcher, who happens to be a super lady and a dog lover herself, phoned me up to tell me about this small white Poodle she had picked up wandering the streets of town. He was an old male dog and since no one came forward to claim him, he was scheduled to be put to sleep at the local veterinarian's. She asked if I would take him. She already had too many dogs of her own to adopt another one, but he was such a little dear and didn't deserve to die. Into town I went, and got the shock of my life when that Poodle turned out to be Odie. He was matted and filthy from having received another year of poor care. I still had to pay the pound fees in order to adopt my own dog who had been stolen from me.

Home I went with him again. It took over six hours of grooming to make him even begin to look like the pretty white Poodle he was. His hair was the colour of mud when I started and I had to trim him right to the skin to get rid of the snarls and mattes. His ears were packed solid with dirty wax and raw from his having scratched so frantically at them. His toenails were long and the ones that had not broken off, jaggedly curled sideways making it difficult for him to walk with any degree of comfort. His teeth were nothing but black stubs from another year of improper diet.

I placed an ad in the city newspaper, asking for a home for him with someone who had a heart as big as gold. I must have interviewed over fifty people over the telephone before finding the person who had the love inside to make Odie's last years good ones. This lady who took him into her home is one of the most wonderful people I have ever met.

Regardless of the cost, she had him neutered and his poor teeth attended to. She said that they were so bad that her vet had to pull all of them but five. Renamed Spike, he does just fine with only five teeth. Happy at last, Spike has finally found the master he, like any dog, deserves. A house to live in, a lap to lie on, and a gentle hand to pat his shining, clean coat. Thank you Marion.

THE FORGOTTEN ONES

There are many definitions for a puppy mill. The registered dog breeders say anyone who breeds anything but registered dogs is a puppy mill. Some say that anyone who breeds dogs for money is a puppy mill. There are many different definitions.

I say that anyone who raises dogs of any size, shape, type or breed is a puppy mill if the people do not love, hold and cherish each and every adult dog on the premises. I say that anyone who does not either keep old dogs past breeding age or does not find them not just any home but a good home, is a puppy mill. Breeders who do not feed, groom and provide medical services, or who starve, beat and fail to provide adequate shelter or who keep the dogs in top form and health but caged and ignored can be accused of running a puppy mill. If people fail to provide love, a gentle hand and some degree of freedom to their charges, but simply breed dogs for profit, then they are a puppy mill.

I have seen these poor creatures in everything from run-down, filthy outbuildings, to heated and air-conditioned kennels. Their eyes beg for love. They quiver with the need for a moment's touch or for a chance to sit on someone's lap, to run free or to frolic with not only their masters, but other dogs. Their whole lives are spent breeding, while they are locked up like animals in a zoo. These dogs are kept in pens where they eat, drink, defecate, get bred, give birth and raise puppies until age brings them down to a bitter cruel end.

I have seen dogs in kennels stacked to the ceiling, know of the hundreds that are used for cruel laboratory experiments and I have seen them in fancy surroundings kept as prize show dogs. One lady raising show dogs couldn't be bothered to call them by name, give them a kind word or even soil her hands by stroking them as they sat in their wire runs, begging for attention.

Living as I do with my pack of four-legged friends has perhaps robbed me of a more normal human existence. I cannot even take a weekend of holidays because in order to give each and every one of them true love on a daily basis takes many, many hours each and every day. On many nights sleep is in short supply while attending births, feeding weak puppies every hour and caring for sick or injured dogs. My life is twenty-four hours a day, seven days a week to assure my friends are truly cared for properly. Add the horses to my daily chores and you begin to see what a full day's work is all about. Now add the fact that I also rescue animals in distress and so much for lying around in the evenings in front of the television.

But I wouldn't change my life for anything in the world. These creatures are not just animals to me but gifts from heaven.

NOIR

I used to always be a big dog person. Meaning, I found small, house dogs as just so many pounds of nuisance. Now that I live in the midst of a pack of these so-called furry nuisances, I wonder how I ever lived without them.

Back then, the bigger, the stronger, the more imposing the dog, the more I liked them. I've changed my preference for dog size, but Noir still remains my all time hero of dogs, my greatest protector, my most faithful of friends.

One year I made arrangements with a neighbour about four miles across country to come and cut and bale my hay for me. Trotting proudly beside his master's tractor as he came up my driveway was a bold, coal black beauty of a dog. He looked to be about a year or so old and resembled a German Shepherd in build. This farmer was at my place about three or four times until the bales were finished and stacked in my yard. Always this magnificent dog accompanied him. Studying the dog, I realized that his conformation was not that of a pure-bred German Shepherd. His chest was too broad, his hindquarters too muscular. He had a smoother coat than a proper Shepherd, and a shorter, more powerful neck. Ringing his entire neck and down into his chest was a thick ruff, seemingly out of place with his short hair coat.

The last day the man was there, curiosity got the better of me and I asked him if the dog was a pure-bred. The man explained to me that he had sold a small farm tractor to a person who raised and trained guard dogs just outside the city of Calgary. Seems this person failed to make good on the final payment on the tractor. After driving to the kennel to attempt to collect the balance owing, he noticed a superb black bitch inside her wire enclosure. Making the comment he might just have to take some of the dogs in lieu of money, he asked about this female. Apparently, she was an imported dog from Belgium. The breeders of this dog were trying to create the ultimate police dog, calling them Belgium Police Dogs (English translation). The breed never did become recognized. The dogs were a cross between German Shepherds and Belgium Sheep Dogs. Six were now in Canada, including this bitch and four of her pups.

One of her eight-month-old pups came home with the farmer and was now standing regally in my yard. Already started in extensive guard dog training, the kennel breeder let him go for two reasons. His coat was too short for their standards and he had a tendency to not listen to all the commands he was given. The farmer had had him for several months now and was quietly telling me I could have the dog if I was to trade my six-month-old Border Collie pup for him. Seems he had never considered the dog to be a trained dog, born and bred as a guard or attack dog, and had tried to teach him to chase and round up cattle. The results were less than satisfactory. The dog had grabbed more than one calf by the throat and thrown it to the ground, rather than nip its heels and chase it into the corral on command. In fact, he had seriously been thinking about doing away with the big brute before he killed any livestock. I traded him on the spot. The Collie pup would be the perfect dog for him.

Never before or since have I owned or loved such a tremendous, proud, faithful companion as Noir.

At a year and a half, Noir was quite a handful. I put him in the garage while the farmer waved goodbye and headed home with the pup riding jauntily in his lap on the tractor seat. Noir leapt onto a workbench and bounced off the small window, high up on the wall. The window cracked. Again onto the workbench, again he hurled himself at the window. Some more cracks. The third time, the glass shattered and he sailed through. Commanding him to stop, he paused long enough to curl his lip at me and was off and running. Cutting across country, he beat the farmer home. The man brought him back in his pickup. I placed him in the barn. Within hours, he literally scratched, clawed and chewed the bottom corner out of the door and went home. I went and got him. I chained him in my yard. He choked himself, leapt and fought hour after hour, chewing frantically on the chain. Finally twisting his mighty neck muscles and off came the collar over his head. The farmer brought him back. I took him in the house with me, fed him tidbits and stroked and pampered him. He ignored me. A friend dropped over and without knocking, opened the door. A black streak shot by him and went home.

Entering his own yard, panting and frustrated, he finds the man's children rolling around on the lawn playing with the Collie pup and not him. Grabbing a garden rake, the man finally was able to beat Noir off the pup before it was killed. Again and again, he chased Noir off the property. Again and again, the dog tried to crawl back, his tail between his legs, crying in confusion, not understanding why he was no longer wanted. He was heartbroken. I went and got him.

He never left my side again. In all the years I had him, he went everywhere with me if at all possible. He devoted himself to me with a fierce desire to belong to me and only me. He also never again tucked his tail between his legs or ever cried out in fear or submission. His heart was broken that day, shattered in pieces. He never again submitted to anyone, including me. I was not his master. In his eyes, we were equals, thrown together to become a team forever.

When he wasn't in the house with me, he lived in the back of my truck. Eventually I purchased an insulated doghouse for the back of my truck and he was in seventh heaven.

Everything was great until I purchased a new truck. My old one was taken in on trade and Noir watched as his house was placed in the new truck. He jumped into the back on command. Off to work, across town, I went. A couple of hours later, I got a phone call to come and get my dog. My old truck was taken into the shop to start cleaning it up for resale, but Noir didn't think anyone had a right to touch my truck, or I should say, his truck. Over to the dealers I went where Noir happily jumped into the new truck. Noir had been seen several times a day checking on the old truck in the sales lot and warning people away from it. This continued until it was finally sold to an out-of-town customer. But, you know, he had my schedule down pat. Because every single day, when quitting time came at my job, he was snoozing where he belonged, in the back of the new truck.

Noir knew he was not supposed to jump out of the truck box without permission. At work, I let the tailgate down, meaning he had permission to get out if he chose to. So, both of the times he did jump out without permission, I lost him. The first time was late at night coming home on a back road. Some white-tailed deer appeared out of seemingly thin air and bounded across the road. I had come to a full stop to let them cross. I never even gave a second thought to Noir and continued on my way. Once home, I dropped the tailgate so he could come and go as he pleased. Figuring he was inside his house, I told him goodnight and went into my house.

Morning came bright and early and I hollered through the screen door for Noir to come for his breakfast. Noir did not come. I stepped outside and really let out a holler. Noir still did not come. As he often foraged quite a ways from the house at night, I wasn't, at first, too concerned. Stopping to think about it though, he had my schedule down pat enough that he was always back by now, wanting to be there when I woke up.

In a panic I realized that Noir must have jumped out of the truck where I stopped to let those deer cross the road. That was several miles away on a back country, gravel road. I tried not to worry because all my neighbours knew and liked Noir. But the farmers and ranchers along that road didn't know him. If you didn't know him, he generally scared the heck out of you at first glance. He was not only big and black, he just had that look about him. Add this to the fact that his top fangs hung out over his bottom lip and people automatically thought he was snarling at them. Some country guy was going to go for his gun. Noir was in trouble.

I peeled out of my yard and shifted into overdrive. The miles fell away behind me. I was fast approaching where I had stopped to let the deer cross. A black lump was lying motionless on the edge of the road. Oh Lord, he had been hit by a passing motorist and killed. Slowing to a stop, I expected the worst. With a yawn, that ebony fool raised his head, stood and stretched to get the kinks out. He strolled to the side of my truck, gazed in the window at me with one of those, "It's about time you came back for me" looks, and gracefully leapt up and over the side of my truck box. I literally cried with relief.

The second time he jumped out without my knowing it, it was nip and tuck that I would ever get him back alive. My girl friend and I were visiting garage sales all day. As she gathered second-hand furniture and other things for her new apartment, my truck gradually filled up with chairs, coffee tables, lamps and you name it. Noir elected to stay in his house and not get stuff piled on top of him. It was late at night before we finished all our business and went home to her place. Then we watched a movie before deciding to face the task of unloading.

I had hauled the last of it into her place before the realization hit me that Noir was no where to be seen. I'd lost my dog again. It was late and I couldn't for the life of me remember every single place we had been that day. I drove around to the places I remembered hoping to see him lurking around, but no such luck.

I spent a restless night on her couch and the search really doubled in the morning. I notified the RCMP to let them know that if someone phoned in about a vicious-looking stray dog that he would not harm anyone unless provoked. The police were not impressed with me, as Noir could be a potential hazard. I phoned the vet where stray dogs were dumped. I phoned the radio station and talked them into putting it over the radio several times a day. And I drove up and down streets, trying to go back to every place we had stopped the truck for any amount of time, the day before. The second day, I put it in the local paper. And then I went home to the farm and the horses who needed to be worked.

On the fourth day he was missing, the call came which made my tears turn from ones of grief to joy. He was alive. He was hungry, thirsty and lost, but alive. Right smack dab on one of the town's busiest streets outside a popular fast-food restaurant. He had been offered food and water but had refused to eat or drink. I had completely forgotten that we had stopped there for takeout. The staff member who phoned said he was lying next to a dumpster, watching day and night, the entrance door I had gone into. Apparently Noir had seen me go in and thought all this time I was still there, so he waited four days for me to come out. He was as happy to see me as I was to see him.

On the occasion when I moved to another town, the truck odometer really got to chalk up the miles. My horses were still at my old address. Day after day, I drove about fifty miles there and back again. Noir making each trip in the back of his truck. Always, after working and feeding the horses, I stopped at some friends' place for a quick chat before heading home.

Wanting to be gone for a couple of nights to a horse show, I made the decision to leave Noir at home with my landlady so he wouldn't be a pest at the show. I asked her to keep Noir in the house until I had been gone for some time. She later told me that he had listened intently to the sound of my truck vanishing in the distance then with a great sigh, had laid down next to the back door and seemed to sulk. After a spell, she decided to take him for a walk. This tiny, very elderly lady proceeded to take a dog who far outweighed her for a quaint stroll. He simply strolled away from her.

She figured he headed out at about two p.m. At shortly after midnight, my friends heard something bumping and thumping outside their bedroom window. The husband got up and peered out the window into the dark, at a giant black head with, as he always tried to tell me, glowing demon eyes looking back at him. Thinking it was a bear or something far more sinister, he almost shot it with a handgun before realizing it was Noir.

In approximately ten hours, Noir had traversed a distance of some fifty miles. Along gravel roads he had only seen from the back of the truck. The vet figured that he had stuck to the gravel road edges most of the way as his feet were cut to ribbons. He was one tired puppy. He was content to stay at my friends' place until the next night when I could come and get him. He didn't bound joyfully into the back of my truck like other times. Instead he insisted that I boost him into the cab of the truck for the ride back home to my place.

As the months and years came and went, Noir became my shadow. If he was not right beside me when I was out in public every person who knew us would immediately ask me where Noir was. Perhaps he was simply in the back of the truck, or some female dog had attracted his attention. It was a well-known fact that if anyone raised their voice to me, even in mock anger, Noir would be instantly between us, growling low in his throat. Should a person keep it up, the thick ruff on his neck would stand up. Then a ridge of hair would rise the full length of his back. Then his pricked ears would flatten and the growl would turn into a fang-dripping snarl. Thank heavens, it never happened or had to happen, because if he ever attacked, he would have easily been able to tear the throat out of a grown man. Yet he was everyone's friend. Noir greeted every person with a quick rub of his magnificent head against their thigh or extended hand.

He absolutely loved little children and played tenderly with them. My niece Rosalind, then three years old, often rode him as if he was a pony. One time I was playing cards with her parents at the kitchen table. We glanced over at Noir and Rosalind at play. She was lying on the rug, kicking and squealing beneath him as he pretended to savagely maul her. Our hearts almost stopped when he opened his massive jaws and literally took her entire head inside his mouth. The wicked fangs never so much as touched her. Except for being wet from drool, she remained unharmed.

Noir was my friend and a breed of his own. We were not master and dog but two equals in life.

ONLY ONE MASTER

In a wolf pack, there is usually only one Alpha dog, or, simply put, only one leader of the pack. More often than not, the leader is a male who through intelligence, strength and ability to dominate the other dogs becomes the boss dog. The other members follow his orders to the letter or receive a savage beating for disobedience.

The rest of the pack have a pecking order with each one knowing his or her place in society. The domesticated dog has only his master and perhaps a family for his own pack situation. A properly socialized dog will often be satisfied with being on the very bottom of this pecking order. The dog will be most respectful of the Alpha figure (his leader and master) in the home. He will also respect each other family member as he places them above himself. Perhaps the husband has become the leader to him, closely followed by the wife. The children will then rank accordingly, with one or all of them being close enough to his level in the pecking order to allow him to frolic and play with them without him having to worry excessively about doing too much wrong, which in the wild would result in him receiving a good mauling to remind him where he stands in the pack.

Rarely will a dog ever snarl at or bite the person he considers his master and leader, anymore than a wolf would in the wild. Another person high up in his personal pack order is generally safe from a show of aggression on his part. A badly socialized dog though, may try to intimidate members of the family, such as children whom he feels are barely above him in status. This is why the majority of dog bites from a family pet happen to children and not to adults. The children's friends or neighbours are at risk from this type of dog because he has even less respect for them and may show aggression because he feels they are beneath him or perhaps that they have no business being around his pack members and personal territory.

The devotion a dog will show his leader and master is quite something. Be the master kind or cruel, the dog is faithful to him. The dog literally exists for his master.

When a person no longer can keep or wants to keep an adult dog, the dog is sold or given away. In a matter of minutes or hours the dog is faced with a heartbreaking situation. His pack members are gone. His territory has been replaced by a new one. Worst of all, his leader is gone. Many dogs are frightened out of their wits. Some will show aggression to anyone coming too close to them. Some are crazed with grief and lie listlessly, their minds tortured.

Over the years, I have purchased many adult dogs. Because I know what they are going through, I leave them alone as much as possible the first day or two. I don't over handle them, thinking I will win their love quicker that way. When they are ready to come to me for petting and belly rubs, I know they are ready to become a member of this new pack, and are ready to accept me as their new master.

A dog secure in his old home will fit in quicker than a dog who has never been totally sure of his status in life. Female dogs usually fit into my home almost immediately. Most males may take a day or two longer, then accept me as their new leader. Then there are special ones. The dogs who can't seem to get over the loss of their master. Brat, my red male Toy Poodle was one such dog.

Brat's master in his old home was the wife and mother of the family. A tragic accident took her life. Although still surrounded by the rest of the family, he lost the will to live himself. His refusal to eat resulted in a stay in the vet clinic where he was fed intravenously. When he was finally able to return home, he had to be forced to continue eating. Although he tolerated the family, he refused to accept anyone else as his master. He became overly yappy and sulky. He did pretty much as he pleased. The husband hated to sell him but could not tolerate the little guy's strange and aberrant behaviour.

The second blow to Brat's fragile world was being sold and coming to live with me. Again he went off his food. I was forced to feed him a liquid diet purchased from my vet to keep his health up. He appeared like a nice tempered guy, and liked to be picked up and held but he made no attempt to accept me as his master. He existed in some sort of limbo, one minute he would do as I asked and the next he would ignore me as if I was just some stranger who happened to be visiting his home. The more I coddled him, the more superior to me he became. Weeks had passed and I felt I was never going to earn his trust and devotion.

Then I purchased another male adult Toy Poodle. As Brat watched me cuddling and playing with the new arrival, something must have clicked in his brain. He jumped down off the back of the couch and came and sat at my feet, staring up at me intently. From then on he was constantly sitting beside me on the floor just staring at me. If I was at the kitchen sink, Brat would be sitting at my feet. If I was in the bedroom, when I opened the door, Brat would be there. Every time I went outside to the horses, the little red dog was right beside me. Now that he was ready to accept me as his master, he had a big job to do. I could be master and he would be the "next in line boss," which meant he had to assert his authority over all the other dogs in my home. One by one he dominated the other dogs with a savage intent. Within two days he had got over his self-imposed slump, became my faithful servant and set himself up as my personal lieutenant. He was now a happy and faithful companion.

I have purchased adult dogs who have accepted me as their new master, and when they have come into contact with their old master, they seem to have no memory of them, treating them as strangers. I have also sold adult dogs who I was sure would never forget me but after accepting their new masters, they seem to either have no memory of me or at most are only politely friendly. Not so with Pongo.

Pongo's first home would have been the breeding kennel that owned his mother and gave him his start in life. Then at approximately seven weeks of age, he went to his second home. Then while still an adolescent teenager, he was sold again, to

Peter. It was Peter who became his true master and leader. I was to learn that the bond between the man and his dog was extremely strong.

Peter and his wife had made the decision to return overseas to a country that Peter had worked in and was drawn back to. He faced the heart-breaking decision to have to sell his two beautiful Dalmatians, Pongo and Pebbles, as taking them overseas was out of the question. Both dogs were still young but mature adults. I paid a good sum for the pair as breeding animals. Peter, himself, called them into my car, and I noticed tears in this big, strong man's eyes as I drove away.

Pretty Pebbles took to me immediately as if I had always been her master. Pongo tolerated me. He obeyed my every command like the dignified gentleman that he was. He came easily to me to be scratched and petted. But he never once let his guard down and would not accept me as his master. His friend, yes, his master, no. He was one of those rare dogs who would only accept one master in his life and that had been Peter.

No longer able to keep this magnificent pair of dogs myself, now I was faced with the dilemma of finding them suitable homes for the rest of their lives. Pebbles with her kind and trusting ways was no problem, as I knew just the young family to give her to. But what to do with Pongo? He was well marked and had perfect conformation. No doubt I could sell him to someone for a decent sum. I could've easily put an ad in the city paper and let him go to the first interested party. But I had grown to love him and I understood that after almost two years I had never replaced Peter. Could he take one more owner? One more new home? One more new set of rules and lifestyle? In my heart I knew the probable answer to those questions was "no." Should I neuter him and try to keep him? Or would he still attack my tiny housedogs like he was doing now? Should I have him put to sleep? For weeks I pondered these questions.

Maybe miracles do happen. I never thought about Peter and his wife Stella. After all, they were long gone, out of the country. That night when the phone rang and I picked up the receiver to hear Peter's voice on the other end, you could say, I was a bit more than surprised. Moments before I had been chatting with Simone, a close friend, about what I should do with Pongo. Peter had never forgotten about his dog. Going through some old papers, he had run across my telephone number. He phoned to see how Pongo was doing, to know that the dog was happy and loved. Peter informed me that he and his wife had ended up, unable to go overseas. Although they had moved, they were still right here in Alberta.

The second he heard about my trying to make a decision about Pongo's welfare, he immediately asked if he could buy him back. I said no, he could not buy him back. Instead, he could have him for free because no one could ever make Pongo happier than he could.

It had been almost two years, so I certainly did not expect Pongo to actually know Peter. At least not immediately. I felt though, that since he had loved Peter once already, then surely he would do so again with time. Peter and I met in a town parking lot half way between our two homes. Within a scarce couple of minutes, Pongo went from treating Peter like a stranger to a dog full of joy over having finally found his master again. You could actually see the recognition in his eyes and actions. Peter was still driving the same car he had owned two years before. When he told Pongo to go to the car, the dog turned and went across the parking lot directly to that car without looking right or left.

After a couple of weeks, Peter phoned to tell me that he and Pongo were very happy. He told me that never again would Pongo ever be sold or given away. Pongo was home where he belonged.

BEAR DOGS

When my friend Barb took on the task of hand-raising a four-day-old orphan pup, she had no clue of what the future would hold. This tiny Australian Shepherd pup would grow up to be a full-sized warrior who would protect her and her other animals with his life if need be.

Gentle-natured Bruiser helped raise another orphan—a tiny lamb, bottle-fed by Barb and licked, nuzzled and cared for by the dog who towered over it. The lamb even did its best to help Bruiser chase cars, even though the pair would get heck from their worried master when caught in the act.

Bruiser's next special friend was a pint-sized pigmy goat. When a neighbour's German Shepherd came slinking around with the idea of making the goat into Sunday dinner, Bruiser came swiftly to the rescue. Exit one chewed up Shepherd. When a family friend came to visit, bringing along a giant Rottweiler, the Rotti only had to make one pass at the bleating goat and Bruiser was on him in a second. It took five men to separate the two fighting dogs. Much smaller and lighter in weight than the Rotti, Bruiser fought with a single-minded determination to protect his friend.

The first time Bruiser put the run on a bear was right on Barb's back lawn, under her bedroom window. She had awakened to a strange snuffling and snorting sound. Thinking someone was trying to scare her, she peeked out the window. There was a black bear with Bruiser coming at it, jaws snapping and hackles raised. He charged the bear, who made a fast getaway into the bush line

Two years later, Barb was again awakened, this time by the sound of a horse screaming in fear. Grabbing a horse halter, Barb, with Bruiser at her side, ran through the midnight darkness. Reaching the corner of a cross fence, her eyes adjusting to the poor light from the moon, she found her five-year-old gelding, J.R., wild-eyed and covered with lather. Slipping between the rails, she stroked the trembling animal. Seconds later, the panicked horse almost went over top of her as a bear's throaty roar deafened Barb. The cranky beast stood not ten feet away. Even as the bear made ready to attack, Bruiser was on him. This time the bear stayed to fight. Outmatched, Bruiser fought on. Fur and blood flying, the gallant dog was ready to die before letting the bear get to Barb. Its not known how long the fight continued before the bear headed back to the bush. Bruiser stumbling over to Barb and J.R. Reaching down, Barb's hands came away, slick with blood. She had to get the horse out of the corner and to safety. She had to get Bruiser to the house. And the bear was coming back, his angry woofs showing he was ready to do battle again.

Leading fourteen hundred pounds of terrified horse, their backs being guarded by the injured dog, they made it to safety. Taking Bruiser into the house, she gasped at what the bear's slashing front claws had done to her precious guardian.

The beast had opened a terrible wound in the dog's neck. One ear was slashed, shredded. Many hours of loving care by Barb and a veterinarian saved Bruiser's life. The worst was the raging fever he developed from infection. The old dog's nose still is an unsightly reminder of his brush with the bear, as it has never quit peeling and looking raw from having such a high fever.

Barb knows that she is alive and uninjured today, only because of the size of her dog's heart and his loyalty to her and the other farm animals.

Sniffer proved that you don't have to be big to be mighty. Weighing about twelve pounds, this Terrier cross loved to harass bears. He didn't really belong to any one person in particular, as he was simply the camp mutt at an oil company's huge base camp.

He lived off kitchen scraps and hung around, loving any attention the men might give him. The bears often hung around, too. Perhaps drawn to the camp from the bush by the smell of food in the air.

Then, one boss man decided to import himself a Karelian Bear Dog. A dog, who supposedly would attack a bear just because he liked to. It took some time and a bit of hassle to finally get his hands on this dog, but he felt sure it was all going to be worth the expense the next time a bear came along.

Sure enough, it wasn't many days before a bear made an appearance out on the camp's spacious lawn. The man unleashed the bear dog and pointed him in the direction of the bear. The dog took one look at the bear and stuck his tail between his legs and headed in the opposite direction, yelping in fear. The man finally managed to catch the scared-silly mutt, and lead him practically up to the unconcerned bear. The dog sat down and refused to budge an inch. Well, short-legged Sniffer had been watching all this hullabaloo and decided he had better show the imported dog how to go about the job of bear hunting.

Without a sound, Sniffer came charging in. Low to the ground, he had his favourite hold on the bear before the bear had a clue what was happening. His jaws were firmly attached to the back of the bear's hind leg. The bear began to spin around in a tight circle attempting to sink his own, larger, more deadly jaws into some part of the twelve-pound fury. As he spun, Sniffer stayed attached, flying around in the circle caused by the bear's spinning. Then the bear sat down abruptly, forcing Sniffer to let go and quickly wriggle out from beneath the bear's rump.

Running around to the head, Sniffer managed to avoid getting side-swiped by a left hook and still take a nip out of the bear's cheek on the way by. With a roar, the bear couldn't decide to attack or run for it. Well, he made a break for the timber and you guessed it, Sniffer went along for the ride, attached to the hind leg again. We were all laughing over Sniffer's antics, except the man who had the bear-killing dog crouched behind him in fear. Pretty quick, Sniffer came with his tongue lolling, back from another successful day's work. Jauntily, he marched up to the other dog, sniffed his rear, turned, raised his leg and soaked the big mutt's hair. The boss man was not impressed to say the least.

I was told a story of another unusual bear dog. Two men were calving heifers one spring and one of the heifers had needed help getting the calf out and into the world. The calf did not survive and the poor heifer was a downer cow, meaning she either would not or could not get up. So every day the two men had to pack feed and water to her in the hopes she would eventually be able to rise. Their cattle dog, a fine Border Collie, always trotted along beside them. Now, a yearling black bear had taken a liking to the dead calf near by, sort of waiting around for it to spoil some in the hot afternoon sunshine, before making a gourmet meal out of it. One day, the bear started to get annoyed with the men's daily visits and he decided to maybe put the run on the men. Well, the Border Collie decided to put the run on the bear instead. The bear headed for a nearby tree and up he went with the Collie firmly attached to his rump. The dog must have been fifteen feet up in that tree still holding on before he finally let go to make a crash landing on the ground.

My friend Ron claims that he has never had a dog tangle with a bear, but he tangled with one himself. He says everything worked out okay though, because he eventually married her. Sorry Charlotte.

SNEAK ATTACK

They say that you're never too old to learn, or that "you can't teach an old dog new tricks." So many sayings, so much contradiction. Now enter one brindled Boxer pup and myself.

First a bit of history on this fine breed of dog. Our modern-day Boxer is actually a descendant of the British Bulldog, developed into a breed for pit fighting and to bait bulls. Bull baiting was a popular but gruesome sport in the United Kingdom in the days of old. The bull, steer or ox was confined in a corral or even sometimes tethered in the town square. Then these dogs were turned loose to harass the poor beast until it was brought to its knees. The dog who showed the most fighting spirit was considered the best of the best. What is called going for the head meant that the dogs, ripping and snarling, would attack, darting in for the best hold possible on the bellowing animal. The usual site would be an ear, or perhaps the cheek or the dewlap swinging down from the animal's throat. The enraged animal, fighting mad from all the pain, would attempt to trample the dogs, or fling them off with a mighty toss of his head. Now the best hold, the one that counted, was if a dog could latch onto the nose itself. Once the fangs were firmly crunched into the tender nose, if the dog had the strength and determination to hold on, he could literally bring the maddened beast down. Choking in its own blood from the torn nose, unable to breathe, bloody froth bubbling from its nostrils, its front legs slowly folded, and it crashed to the ground. The men then rushed in to cut its throat and the battle was over. Fresh beef would be on the supper table surrounded by much bragging on whose dog took the firmest hold and was the bravest in the attack. The dogs themselves were often seriously injured with broken ribs and limbs and smashed skulls. Thank heavens, the cruel sport lost favour and fell by the wayside. And thank heavens, the Boxer breed that was developed over many years in Germany, became an animal much valued as a spirited pet and guardian of home and family, not a fighting machine out for blood.

Living on a ranch, working cattle daily, often with the help of a sleek Border Collie or wily Blue Heeler, is a grand way to make a living. The dogs often doing the majority of the herding all by themselves with little or no commands from their human masters. The dog coming in low to the ground, behind the beast, a quick nip on the tender heels and the cow heads in the desired direction. Racing around to the front of the cow to turn her if need be. Once the cattle learn what a cowdog is all about, they soon learn to be rounded up with a minimum of fuss.

I was living and working on a cattle ranch, with only Sneakers, my young male Boxer pup who desperately wanted to help me. The trouble was, he was born and bred to not get behind those half-wild range cows, but to go for their heads. The trouble also was that when you almost have that rank cow up to and through the corral gate, and your dog comes out of nowhere and takes a nip out of her nose, things can get a bit hectic. Chances are that your cow doesn't make it through the gate. Chances are your dog, running gleefully back to you, with a ticked off cow hot on his tail, makes you wish you were somewhere else.

So, on a whim, I set out to teach Sneakers to be a cowdog. The days turned into weeks and then into months, but slowly he learned to leave the head alone, to go for the heels instead. The hardest part for Sneakers was learning that if he came in low and the cow kicked, she would kick over top of him and not hit him. At first he took quite a beating, sometimes a dozen whammies in one afternoon. He never did learn to crouch down; instead he sort of perfected a technique of nipping and dropping down on his right side. He started to be pretty darn good at putting them where I wanted them to go. He even learned to bark only when needed instead of the whole day long.

It was looking like it was about time to let other people know that I had myself a trained Boxer cowdog. I started to brag just a bit to everyone about my Sneakers. Those old cowboys just sort of shook their heads and humoured me by listening to my tales.

It was the last load of grass yearlings to head up the loading chute into the back of the cattle liner. It was Sneakers and my chance to prove his worth as a cattle dog. As dusk fell, darkness was coming up fast and those cattle needed to be loaded. Ordering my dog to start nipping heels under the bottom rail of the long chute, I waited for those cattle to load in record time. The first few started up the ramp and I turned away for a split second to close a gate when all hell broke loose. The cattle already in the liner were bellowing and trying to stampede back down over top of the others. Then one steer in the liner really went on the fight. By the light from the truck driver's flashlight, it didn't take long to see why. Sneakers had a firm hold on his nose. The dog had quit coaxing the heels in the chute, and instead had leapt into the back of the liner and reverted to his ancestors' way of going for the head. The steer was smashing him around in there and Sneakers was holding firm. I let a blood-curdling yell out of me and Sneakers realized his master was apparently a tad upset. He let go and dove between crashing hooves to get out of there. My second yell sent him scurrying like a whipped pup back to the house.

Well, as you may have guessed, getting those cattle straightened around and reloaded was no easy task. You may also be able to guess that I didn't do a whole lot of bragging about my new breed of cattle dog either. Those old cowboys just nodded their heads and said I told you so when the story got around. Hey, he was tough though, a really spirited pet and a fine guardian of home and family.

SUCH A SHORT EXISTENCE

It was to be my third night in a row with little or no sleep with another one of my pregnant dogs having reached her birthing time. My days, filled with the feeding, care and responsibilities of not only dogs, but the horses as well, had made me quite tired from the lack of quality sleep. I was even beginning to doubt my ability to care and live in the same house as all these little ones. This girl's birthing pen was in the living room. A four-foot square pen that you have to side pass to turn on the television or answer the phone. With a long look at the comfortable couch, I sat down on the end of the coffee table, knowing that if I laid down for even a second, I would fall fast asleep. I straightened my spine and prepared myself for observation without sleep.

Four tiny ones entered the world without difficulty. A quick check of my girl told me at least one more baby waited to be born. As unlikely as I thought, I must have dozed off sitting upright on a hard, narrow coffee table. Something woke me. Perhaps the sounds of the mother dog licking and cleaning her last new-born.

I opened my eyes to see that she had broke the sac and chewed through the umbilical cord. She had also immediately pushed it away from her out of the nest, something a good mother dog will do with a dead pup or if something is wrong with it. Mother Nature tells her to do this.

Quickly, I scooped up the rejected puppy. It was motionless but still warm. It was not too late to try and save it. In seconds I had gone through the motions of clearing its air passages. I roughly massaged its rib cage. A quick glimpse showed it to be a girl puppy. Still she did not draw a lung full of much needed air. Instantly I placed her wet little muzzle between my lips to gently blow life saving oxygen into her lungs. Gently, but with an urgent determination, I gave her the same CPR anyone would give a human child. She gasped, mouth gaping wide. I kept on. Her breathing stabilized. Finally, she gave a cry of outrage at my unwanted administrations. Finally, she squirmed, twisted and turned, already looking for her mother's breast. I took a few seconds longer to dry her coal black coat. Exhausted, I found myself smiling. I raised her one last time to my lips to give her a good luck kiss before placing her with the other four brothers and sisters.

I think I almost had a heart attack at that instant because for the first time, I saw her delicate puppy face was horribly disfigured. Her jaw was not aligned. One eye was lower than the other. One ear was fused to her skull.

Her mother had pushed her aside for a reason. Mother Nature knew. I had just spent desperate minutes saving the unsaveable.

Choking back my own cry, I knew what must be done. Sick, right down to my very soul, I knew that she could not survive. I knew what I must now do. To give life and turn around and take it away. I had no choice. Holding her close against my breast, I left her mother and healthy siblings. I was so tired. I was so alone.

BEST FRIENDS

Dogs can and do form extremely close bonds with other species of animals. Jean's dog and cat had grown up together and were inseparable. They went everywhere together, the dog often slowing his pace so the cat could catch up with him. When at rest, they would lie together and, with their two little tongues licking like crazy, groom each other. The cat usually ended up pretty wet and slobbery looking.

Jean came home from working for me one afternoon to find her dog missing. The rope he had been tied with had broken leaving at least ten feet still attached to his collar. Pussy Cat was of course missing too, obviously having gone with the dog. Jean searched until dark and for another three long days to no avail.

Then the cat came home—thin, tired and meowing like crazy. He paced back and forth on the lawn. He did not want to be taken into the house, so Jean fed him on the doorstep. The minute he was done eating, instead of resting and grooming himself, he yowled at Jean and began to walk away. Quickly she followed him.

The brambles and bush tore at her clothing and scratched her face and arms. If she fell behind too far, the cat would sit down and wait for her, his yowls filled with desperation. Down a coulee bank, Jean slipped and slid following him. Then the cat led her right to the entangled dog. The rope was wrapped around a deadfall of old broken branches and roots.

Gaunt with hunger and thirst, the dog nuzzled the tired cat who had laid down between his front legs. He was saved by his best friend who had returned home to find help and lead their human back to him.

When I purchased my registered Quarter Horse stallion, Skiddor, I also purchased a three-month old German Shepherd-Husky cross named Blaze. A long yearling, Skiddor was used to having a lot of horses his age to play with. And young stud colts love to play. Now, here he was at my place with no one to be his buddy. He was lonely and so was the pup.

They formed a very close bond. The huge colt could easily have seriously injured or killed Blaze, but as they leapt, bounded and frolicked, Skiddor's flashing front hooves, mighty kicking hind legs and savage teeth seemed to stop just short of doing any harm.

The big colt seemed to become more dog-like with each passing day. Blaze taught him to play tag and tug-of-war. What a sight! With the dog on one end of an old burlap feed sack, and Skiddor on the other, they tugged and pulled each other back and forth. Blaze would pick up anything he could—an old glove, a piece of rope, even good sized sticks—and take them into the horses pen where his friend and him could chew, wave around and fight over them.

They even ate together. Blaze took a liking to rolled oats twice a day, burying his head alongside Skiddor's in the feed bucket. Should one of them go to the trough for a drink of water, the other one was always immediately thirsty. They often slept together in the deep straw in Skiddor's shed. The big colt stretched out on his side with the dog curled up tight against him. They were buddies, as close as brothers.

Spring rolled around and Skiddor was about to become a breeding stallion. I had booked ten mares to him even though he was only a two-year-old. He was well developed and rapidly showing interest in the opposite sex. Blaze didn't take kindly to his friend's interest in those mares. In fact, he went totally off the deep end over it.

The first time I went to breed a mare with the colt, Blaze's jealousy got the best of him. He tried his best to distract the horse with leaps and bounds, clearly saying, "Hey buddy, forget that homely old mare, come play tag." Skiddor acted as if Blaze no longer existed. Frantically Blaze ran out to the pasture and brought back a tree branch to play with. Skiddor never even noticed. In desperation from being ignored, the silly dog took a bite out of the colt's rear leg. Never before had he bit his friend. Suddenly his friend was a kicking, mad demon.

I caught the dog and tied him up. Blaze choked himself and howled in anguish. It was too much for the horse to handle. He lost all interest in the mare, turning around to neigh at the dog, worried over the sounds the dog was making.

I took Blaze into the house and locked him in the bathroom. Skiddor could still hear his friend begging and pleading to come rescue him. He simply could not concentrate on the job at hand, turning to stare at the house and snorting and blowing.

I thought the world of that silly dog, but this friendship was going to have to end. I gave Blaze away to a friend of mine, and I swear the horse missed him as much as I did. Without Blaze to play with, he eventually returned to being a normal horse, instead of fourteen hundred plus pounds of over-grown Poodle.

BOB AND ANN TO THE RESCUE

It had been a long night. My dog, Mandy, had not been feeling well and had chosen my bedroom closet to hole up in. Her restlessness kept her tossing and turning through most of the night. Each time she thumped against the wall, all my ghosties from when I was a little girl made me jump in bed, sure that some unknown evil lurked just inside that closet, waiting for me to fall asleep. I had already had a late night looking for my Polly dog who had disappeared that afternoon and no amount of calling had made her come galloping in from the field. You can imagine that with the arrival of the morning sun creeping into my bedroom window, I was fair tired and grumpy. Mumbling and complaining, I got dressed and opened the bedroom door to start another day. Mandy, feeling much better, shot past my legs heading for the bathroom. She was forced to zig around Polly who had returned and was laying in front of the bedroom door with her tail wagging in greeting. She was holding her catch of the night between her front paws. Not in the best of moods, I told Polly that it was a pretty poor trophy she was offering me. After missing all those hours, she should have produced more than one scrunched, half grown, skinny mouse. Poor Polly. Tired, worn out, wet and mud-caked, she had done her best to bring scavenged food to me, almost nightly, but this day I was not pleased. Worse, I fired her prize catch into the garbage without even giving her a pat on the head. She watched with sad eyes, as I stomped into the bathroom and closed the door.

I hurried my morning shower, you might say barely getting wet from head to toe. Feeling refreshed, I threw open the bathroom door. I heard the sound of galloping dog feet and watched a panting Polly hurl herself through the outside doggie door with a look of pride on her chubby face. With her tail waving, she came to me and dropped her offering at my feet. One fat, big mouse. Nothing skinny about this one. Nothing dead about it either. I guess in her hurry to bring me a trophy I would be proud of, she just didn't have time to kill it first. My Cockapoo Racey's snapping jaws took care of the mouse while I made double sure to tell Polly what a good hunting dog she was and give her two pats on the head. After all, not every Maltese-Poodle cross can hunt like my Polly dog.

I went back to the living room to check on Blackie who was due to give birth, probably sometime today. Blackie greeted me with her whole rear end wagging. Her tail gets going first with such enthusiasm, the whole dog seems to start wagging. She asked to be let out to go to the bathroom and I obliged.

Wanting to check early on my neighbours' mare that I was caring for while they were away for the weekend, I jumped in the car and headed for their place a couple miles away. She was due to foal anytime now. I had checked her the night before and noted that even though she was close, I figured one more day at least. Sure enough, she was fine. But their two dogs were not. Both sprouted mustaches of porcupine quills. Their sad eyes and faint whines pleading for help. Promising them I would be right back with the pliers and someone to help hold them, I tore back down the road to home.

I had only been gone a few minutes and the first thing I did when I jumped out of my car, was try to find Blackie to put her back in the safety of the living room, because she was closer to birthing than the mare was. No Blackie! Whenever a dog goes missing I always start my search in the horse corrals. There is always the fear that my little mutts aren't answering my call because a horse has trampled them. No Blackie. She was going to have pups and soon. So I searched the outside dog houses, the farm buildings and knelt down to call under them. No Blackie!

Bob and Ann to the rescue. Dear friends that they are, they came immediately from their home in town to help me anyway they could. Ann began her search around and behind the bale stacks, Bob also began checking the horse pasture and corrals for Blackie. I went to my old granary to mix the morning feed for the horses, once that chore was out of the way, I could help in the search. Bending over a sack of grain, I heard a faint peeping noise. Stopping to listen, I heard it again. The unmistakable sound of a just born puppy. Calling Bob and Ann, we pinpointed the whereabouts of the sound—directly under our feet. Blackie was giving birth in the few inches of space beneath that old building. Already there was enough peeping and squeaking to indicate at least three new-borns. With a flashlight, Ann was able to locate her exact position from the red flash of her eyes in the sudden light. Bob got to work, shovelling inside the bin until he had a space cleared down to the floorboards. Quickly he worked to loosen and tear up a board directly over top of the dog and her babies. Good thing too, because as I lifted the new-borns from their mother's hastily dug hole in the wet, dank earth, water from the melting spring runoff was already trickling towards their nest.

With the mother and her babies safely back in the house, the three of us headed for the neighbours' to try our luck at removing quills. Now, Wayne and Lorraine's farm dogs don't know us, so basically we are intruders. Intruders trespassing on their turf and we are going to help them by causing them a fair amount of pain when we extract each quill, one at a time, over and over again.

First, the three of us petted the dogs and let them get to know us a bit. Then it was time. With Bob and Ann holding onto the male, I started pulling quills. What a sweetheart of a dog. As each quill was extracted, he winced but made absolutely no attempt to bite. Good thing too, because being a Kuvasz, a giant of a dog, weighing well over a hundred pounds and standing about as high as a small Shetland Pony, I'm sure one bite would have been the end of me. Having finished on the outside of his muzzle, I opened his mouth to check inside. I felt like a circus lion tamer about to put my head inside the lion's mouth. I'm sure my head would have fit nicely inside those gaping jaws, but I settled for just eyeballing the interior instead. Lion tamer I was never cut out to be. One in his tongue and a couple on the roof of his mouth. Warning Bob and Ann that this was going to hurt the dog more so than pulling them out of his lips and nose, I quickly yanked the one out of his tongue. That big old dog, simply stood up and walked away, carrying Bob and Ann with him like a couple of pesky flies who just happened to be sitting on him. We repeated this with the last of the quills, and turned him loose, one of the gentlest dogs I have ever worked with.

Now for the female Border Collie. She must have jumped right on that ole porky because even her chest and inside her front legs were full of quills. One by one we pulled them and opened her mouth to check. She looked like a pincushion in there. Again I was amazed at her allowing this to go on. I figured that if she started to snap and fight I would have to take her to my vet to get those quills out of her tender tongue and roof of her mouth. With each quill pulled, she yelped and struggled in their grasp but never once did she go on the fight. Her poor tail continued to wag frantically, her eyes pleading with us to hurry up and turn her loose.

Thank heavens for my friends. People like Bob and Ann, make it so that I can keep on going. They are always there when push comes to shove. They are there when my dogs and horses prove that one person, alone, just plain sometimes needs a helping hand.

WOLF HYBRIDS

I find it very amusing to be scanning the "Dogs for Sale" columns in the newspapers and see ads such as "Half Wolf Pups for Sale," or "Wolf, Husky Cross Pups for Sale." If you phone these ads and ask explicitly where and how the wolf enters the picture in the dog's pedigree, these are the most typical conversations you will have:

"The mother is part wolf."

"Oh, from her mother or her father's side?"

"I don't know, that's what the guy told me who gave her to me, that she is part wolf."

So I got the name and number of the previous owner and gave him a call.

"Yah, she is half wolf, the female they got off me."

"Oh, who is the wolf, her mother or her father?"

"The father is."

"So you bred her to a wolf?"

"Yah, well, she came into heat and took off from the farm and came back bred and gave birth to these wolf puppies."

"So you never actually saw the father?"

"Nope, but they don't look like the neighbours' mutts very much, so it had to have been a wolf who bred her."

"Hello, I'm phoning about the half wolf pups you have for sale. Who is the wolf, the mother or the father?"

"The father is."

"Oh, you own a wolf?"

"Well, no, actually it's the neighbours' dog who is almost a wolf, he looks exactly like one."

"Oh, I see, I guess where you live you must see a lot of real wolves in the wild, pretty close up too so you can study them?"

"Don't be silly, all you ever catch is a quick glimpse of a wild wolf."

I have yet to speak to a single person running one of these ads who can prove that the dogs they own are part wolf.

Over the years, I have read every piece of material I could get my hands on about wolves. Simply because these wondrous creatures fascinate me. I have learned, mostly from information compiled by experts, that wolves do not make good pets. It is not because of the falsehoods that people believe about wolves being vicious animals, it is because it has been bred into them to exist in a rigid pack situation. When kept with humans, the humans replace other wolves in the pack. Now the wolf must spend his entire life trying to figure out where he stands in the pack. Perhaps he can use his fangs to move up a notch in the hierarchy of the pack. Maybe he can even become leader of the pack over the other members. The human members of the pack could be about to get savagely mauled by their pet wolf who has always been so timid. He didn't go insane, he just picked today to become leader of his pack. Most wolves are actually very timid creatures except when hunting and pulling down prey for their supper. Hunting is a different story entirely.

Crossing dogs and wolves has been done for many, many years by first trappers and later sled dog racers, in order to put more stamina and endurance into their teams. These are working dogs, not pets. They were never intended to be some family's pet. They are indeed part wolf and may, in a stressful situation, react like the wolf hybrid they are. With unpredictability. Do you really want this animal around your children?

Time and time again, I have seen a Husky or Malamute-type dog, called part wolf simply because they resemble a wolf in colouring, hair coat and size. When I first laid eyes on Fellow, I thought he was just a regular dog until I studied his tail carriage and skull. Along with the owner's account this half wolf added up to being the real McCoy. I was at an animal shelter to try to rescue this four-year-old from a date with death.

Male wolves don't just jog into human territory and breed what they would consider a lowly female dog. Even if they thought about it, wise to the ways of man, they tend to stay well out of gunshot range. Female wolves don't just suddenly get over their fear and hatred of man and his dogs and come looking for a male dog to marry up with them. It is a different story though when a man captures and raises a wolf.

Fellow came from a remote village in the Northwest Territories. His mother was an Arctic Wolf who had been trapped as a pup. She was kept chained all her life to the trapper's cabin. When she came into heat, the man crossed her with a sled dog. *Voilà*, real half wolf pups.

This man from Alberta was employed by the government in the Territories and came home with Fellow. The wolf dog ended up spending his life chained in this man's back yard. Frustration from the close confinement resulted in his continued howling. The man then would get complaints from the neighbours, go out and kick and beat the dog. Being unable to escape the beatings resulted in the ninety-some pound dog finally turning on his owner and putting him in the hospital with several wounds that would leave the man badly scarred for life.

Fellow was then picked up by an animal control officer and his days were numbered. So there I was, talking up a storm, begging to be allowed to try and rehabilitate the dog. Home I went with my new, I hoped, soon to be friend.

Because I lived in the country, they had agreed to release him to me. Along with the dog came a mess of fleas, ticks and you name it. Tying him tight to the fence, I went for a can of louse powder. Talking softly to him, I explained that I wasn't going to hurt him, only dust him down to the skin with the powder for his own good. Fellow promptly ripped the sleeve of my coat wide open. Maybe, he enjoyed his creepy crawlies more than I realized.

Within a few days, Fellow seemed to start liking my company, so the two of us headed to Mr. Tweed's where I rented horse pasture. Once there, Fellow stayed within calling distance while I took a ride on a green horse I was training. Mr. Tweed was a retired farmer who didn't ask for much in life. He had a steer he was fattening for the deep freeze and a couple of old, scrawny hens that laid him an occasional egg. Fellow devoured the first poor old hen without a peep out of her. The second hen managed to let out one pretty good squawk before biting the dust.

Hearing that squawk had me off the horse and heading for the chicken coop. Without thinking, I shouted at Fellow and grabbed him by the thick ruff on his neck. In a flash, he had dropped the chicken and had me by the arm. He just stood there, applying intense pressure with his rather large teeth and growling a warning. Knowing I had made a serious mistake in going so suddenly at the dog, I just stood motionless, not saying a word. After a few seconds, he released his hold on me and ignoring the chicken's warm body, strolled outside and jumped into the back of my truck. Although my arm would remain a nice deep purple for several days, I was amazingly unhurt.

I took Fellow everywhere with me. He enjoyed the freedom I so often gave him. He gloried in being able to stretch into a full run, to leap and bound. The day I attended a local rodeo with him, he proved that he was still a wolf in dog's clothing. First the calf shot out into the arena, followed by the cowboy and his horse, the loop in the man's rope ready to catch the calf, then Fellow came out of nowhere. He caught the calf first by the throat, dragging it down with sheer size and strength. The audience was on their feet screaming "Wolf! Wolf!" I jumped the fence and raced towards the dog. Fellow released his supper and stood daring me to discipline him.

In only a month or so of owning him, I knew that I had been lucky so far with this majestic beast. I also knew that one day my luck would run out. I finally found an elderly bachelor who lived way out in the country, miles away from any other people or livestock, who would care for the dog and let him run free.

My friend Linda has had me laughing and crying over some of the remarkable dog stories she has told me. One of my favourites was of her sister, Wendy, who is a true dog lover. Also she is someone who has owned a wolf-dog cross. Actually two of them. The first one was a splendid creature but alas did not live very long. It was run over by a truck on the farm. Even more sad was the dog's passing away on Christmas Eve, which is also Wendy's birthday.

Her next wolf hybrid was one very lucky dog. Not so lucky when terribly injured as a wee pup still nursing its mother, but lucky that this kind girl chose to give her not only a home but several operations to make her life whole.

There were seven pups in the litter. By accident the heat lamp, hung above them to keep them warm, was knocked loose and ended up down in the straw. It set the kennel on fire. Four little ones perished. Two escaped injury and Pippin was horribly burned. Kind-hearted Wendy chose this pup over the uninjured ones.

Pippin simply loved everybody and anybody. Even the veterinarian who operated time and again on her to eventually give her less burn scars. Joyfully wagging her tail, Pippin never hesitated to leap gracefully up onto the vet's examination table. This silver-coloured half wolf knew only kindness and love. She returned these sentiments tenfold.

ANIMAL TALK

Animals know how to communicate with us if we take the time to listen. I once found a starving young magpie who had fallen out of her mother's nest. I took her home, against my father's wishes, and fed and cared for her. She talked silly things to me, bobbing her head and telling me all her troubles.

Michael, my family's pet crow, would wait patiently either on top of the propane tank near the back door or on the roof of the house I grew up in. The second the door was left open for more than a second, in Michael would fly. His destination was the butter dish, always left on the dining room table. Swooping down, he knew he had only a quick second to plunge his beak, wide open, into that butter. Then my irate mother would be hot on his case. Mom would chase him back out the door, with his beak stuffed wide open, full of home-made butter, Michael hopping along on the floor, Mom hopping mad.

Michael did not just eat the butter, he took the glob and neatly deposited it on top of the propane tank. Then with loving care he took tiny bits of it and preened every feather on his body. As you might be able to guess, he smelled quite strongly of rancid butter.

Mom had managed to capture me one glorious summer day and was making me help her in our home. As an aspiring young bronc rider, I wasn't happy to be doing house work, instead of out riding my horses. With Mom fussing and me plugging along, we suddenly could hear Dad laughing like a total maniac out in the yard. He laughed and he laughed. In fact, he was laughing entirely too much and for too long. Mom soon figured out that the long days of farming, the unpaid bills and the hot, hot sun had finally toasted his brain.

Slowly, we snuck out of the house to see if he was too far-gone to be safe! Well, it wasn't' Dad, it was that silly crow,

Michael. There he sat, on top of the big farm gas tank, imitating Dad's laugh to the best of his ability. No wonder we thought Dad's laugh was just a bit too crazy and not totally normal.

Many years later, I was to fall totally in love with two young crows that I had rescued from a building scheduled for demolition, and had made pets out of them. These extremely intelligent birds were the world to me. Aptly named Dirty Bird (he simply could not be house trained) and just plain Crow, they were the joy of my life. Although they talked nonsense to me as my pet magpie had done, Dirty Bird did finally learn to say his name. Not that it was perfect, you understand. He would gesture frantically for attention, saying his name, *Irdy Ird, Irdy Ird*.

But this is not what I mean by animal talk.

My stallion, Skiddor, communicates with me every day, especially during breeding season. I spend hours hand breeding and working alone with him, developing a close bond between us. He is incredibly intelligent and knows several human word commands such as, his nick-name, "Skiddor." He knows to "Come" to me on command, to "Get Back," to "Whoa" and to "Quit Being a Jerk." But most of our communication is silent. I know when he is mad or upset, and he knows when I'm mad or upset. I know when he wants to be loved, stroked and petted, and he knows when I need a friendly nudge from his silky nose.

But I still haven't fully explained animal talk.

Nobody, neither human nor bird or any other animal can quite make their way into my heart like a dog. All dogs, big or small, male or female, young or old, speak to me.

Tiffany sits on the other side of the flaps to the dog door and cries. She knows that the best way to get my attention and get picked up is to sit out on the step and cry, as if she can't get in.

Tari Tari loved to be in my bedroom, but without all the other dogs. She would pretend to hear something outside, go nuts convincing the rest of the pack to go hunt down the intruder. Then knowing full well they were off on a wild goose chase, she would get to curl up alone with me.

If my Sammy dog would see me grooming another dog, she would act like a cat, licking the inside of her paw and grooming her face until I came and groomed her.

Bailey, who is some spoiled, always gets the last bite of whatever meal I'm eating. If I forget and swallow that last bite, she gets down off my lap and paws frantically at one of the dogs' dry food bowls. Apparently that last bite would have kept her from starving to death.

My little dog actually smiles at everybody and everything, until I tell her, "You are such a mutt." Then she pouts, big time. No smile now as she knows full well she is too cute to be just a common mutt.

Rusty, when she thinks she is lacking in attention, grabs a firm hold on my pant leg and refuses to let go until I stroke her.

Fleecy threatens the other dogs with snapping and snarling, but only when I'm there to protect her for she knows that without me as her guardian, she will get savagely mauled.

But still I'm not saying it right. It is their eyes, watching me, seeing inside my very soul. How when I am having an off day, perhaps a headache day, they are so quiet and you hardly know they are there. When I'm having a "I think I'm going to win the lottery day" they are so jubilant, they never quit barking and leaping and playing. They talk to me without sometimes so much as an audible sound. They talk to me with their actions and their deeds.

SHE GAVE UP

Margo Morton had always wanted one of the most glorious of dogs—a Siberian Husky. These dogs are proud, agile and beautiful to behold. With a bit of wheeling and dealing, Margo finally purchased a Canadian Kennel Club registered beauty. His grey wolf coat was magnificent. His limbs were straight and true. She marvelled at her good luck in now owning him. With a sturdy collar and chain, she tethered him next to the house.

After a quick bath, Margo dropped the kids at their grandparents' and went to a baby shower she had to attend. The first of her bad luck was about to unfold. Her husband was the first one to arrive, in the dark, to their home deep in bush country. In the glare of his headlights, he came to a rolling stop next to the house believing that he saw a wolf lurking there. Normally you only catch a glimpse of wolves in the bush, perhaps loping along a cut line, not boldly standing next to your house. Margo's husband feared something was wrong with this wolf, that he must be rabid or crazy, because he was just standing there, not slinking off into the bush. One shot from the rifle finished the wolf.

It took a while for Margo to try again, but finally she purchased a glorious red Siberian named Cruise. Margo's intentions were to show him vigorously, to make him a champion. Bad luck, number two. His testicles were not descended, which meant that he could not be shown—it's against the rules. With a sigh, Margo got him neutered. She paid the vet bill and promised to love him forever, even though her dreams of a champion were put on hold.

Never a quitter, she bided her time and finally purchased a silver grey bitch, a beautiful female with what we call "presence."

Hoping things would now be different, Margo hired a lady to show Angel. In a matter of months, she buried her face in the thick coat of her Canadian Kennel Club champion. It had cost many, many dollars but it had been well worth the expense, for now she had a champion, who, when bred to a stud dog with champion bloodlines, would make her nothing but profit. Payback time.

Over the next months, years, she made the long drive to the stud dogs of her choice. Four times she paid the costs and totalled up the miles. Bad luck number three was about to make itself all too clear. Angel would not catch. Many vet bills later Margo was informed that her pretty Angel would never give her a litter of pups. Margo would probably not see any return on her dollar, but she had Angel and loved her and that was all that mattered.

At seven years old, Angel had the run of the land, her joy in life expressed in leaps and bounds. The neighbours down the road had a mutt male that decided to come visiting. No human thought to tell these two creatures that they couldn't get married. Their marriage was short and sweet. Margo put the run on him seconds after they had their honeymoon. Thank heavens, Angel couldn't have puppies or Margo might have been really upset.

Bad luck number four was about to make itself all too apparent. This champion Husky was in pup to the neighbours' mutt. In labour far too long, a caesarean had to be performed to have five mutt puppies. Then back to the vet when she went into a life-threatening state of shock. The vet bills piled up and because of her complications, Angel had to be spayed at the same time as the caesarean. Margo's dreams of raising champion Siberians had pretty much gone right out the window.

Margo's policy is, "never give up." Well, I must say, after bad luck, number one, she bounced back. After bad luck number two, she did a lot of soul searching. After number three, she really started to mumble under her breath. Number four, pretty well toasted her desire to raise, show and train these special dogs. But, hey, she has Cruise, pretty Angel, and a fine looking yearling pup from Angel's litter named Tipperary. He sort of looks Siberian. Sort of.

TARI TARI

When I write about dogs, in particular rescued dogs, my thoughts always turn to my poor Tari Tari. She would never be far from me when I was in the house. If she caught me looking at her, she would point her muzzle straight in the air and give me one of her growl barks. It was a sound from deep within her soul, a sound like no other dog I have ever owned. Some, I suppose, would find it an annoying, sharp sound. To me, it was music to my ears, music for my soul.

I rescued her with the idea I would get her in healthy shape, both physically and mentally, and place her in a good adoptive home. But Tari Tari never left me.

She had had no life. She came from a puppy mill and was held back for breeding purposes. She had never known from birth a kind hand, gentle arms to hold her or a pat of affection. She was born and raised in a stinking, dirty garage with little food and water, and was probably never spoken to and never touched. She was just a dog meant to be born, mature, be bred and give birth until she could no longer produce and would then be put down when she was no longer a money maker for her uncaring owner.

A lady phoned me and told me the terrible conditions a woman was keeping her dogs in. She had tiny lap dogs—Poodles, Malteses, Poms, Shih-tzus and Llasa Apsos—all crowded into this garage that was sweltering hot in the summer and without heat in the winter. The kind lady was trying her darnedest to get the SPCA to do something about this situation. The staff of the SPCA are often overwhelmed with the task of checking every complaint and everything else that they must do to help our poor creatures in need. The laws bind their hands, making their jobs all the harder. Because this person in question supplied pet stores with cheap puppies, she was able to continue to operate, but apparently was not making ends meet, so she was trying to sell some of the older dogs for additional income. The wonderful lady who phoned me had taken the one she felt needed the most help. Another friend of hers had paid to take another. And I took Tari Tari.

She was supposed to be a pure-bred Maltese. I raise what I consider to be the best of cross-bred dogs there are. This frightened, never before out of her pen, shaking, one-year-old female was obviously not a pure-bred Maltese but a Malti-Poo, half Maltese and half Poodle.

I got her to her proper weight for her size at about seven pounds. When I first took her home she weighed in at three and three-quarter pounds. So pathetically thin, just a skeleton covered with hair. There is no doubt in my mind that she had never been picked up or if she had been, probably by the scruff of her neck. This poor creature scrunched herself down on the passenger side of my truck seat for the ride home. She shook so violently for the entire three-hour trip that I thought she would literally just give up and die of a heart attack on me. Eyes wild with fright, panting with fear and the unknown awaiting her. Halfway home, I stopped and got her a take out cup of water. Holding it, I slowly stretched my hand out to her. Seeing my hand coming she actually screamed in fear like an injured rabbit.

To calm her, I tried singing softly to her on that trip home. Now, I can't sing diddly squat at the best of times, but while making up silly things to sing to her, I came up with her name. I had asked the woman who had owned her what her name was and was told, "Name? I don't have time to give these #*%#*% things names, geez all they do is cost me money. Take her, give me your money and no receipt." I don't remember what I tried to sing to her that afternoon, I only know she became Tari Tari.

Now, my fur-covered buddies are always excited to see me when I arrive home, even if I've only been gone twenty minutes. On this day I was gone seven or eight hours, and when I arrived with a new addition to the pack with me, all tarnation broke loose. I always carry the new member of the house in with utmost care, and place them in a kennel in the kitchen so that everyone can smell noses through the door and no blood is shed. Once the pack calms down, I can take the latest arrival out, hold them in my lap and let everybody get acquainted.

Tari Tari gave every indication that she was not used to being picked up, let alone held in somebody's arms. Out of fear, she urinated on me and even passed a small amount of stool, all out of total fear.

I think I knew then that this was most definitely the worst case of neglected dog I had ever encountered. The others might have been abused, might have been undernourished, might have known a terrible life in some respect but not like this. We are talking a mature dog here who simply did not know human touch, let alone kindness.

Getting to know Tari Tari was painstakingly slow. For her it must have been a thousand times worse. She had obviously never been in a clean, poop-free environment before, let alone in a house. Even though I have a dog door leading straight outside to total freedom without fences or boundaries out here in the country, she refused to go outside. Even though I have a porch half-covered in newspaper for those who think they can't quite make it outside, she thought you just ate, drank, pooped and slept in the same spot. She just didn't know any other way to exist. Being a shy dog, she was happy just having her corner of the kitchen to do everything in.

Slowly, carefully, I got to know her. Gently, I would pick her up when I saw her defecating on her blanket where she slept and push her out the dog door. It took time, but eventually, she learned that going to the bathroom either outside or on the newspaper in the porch was just so much better than on her blanket.

Slowly, she began to trust me. Or should I say, she wanted with all her heart and soul to trust me. Frightened of being picked up didn't help matters. It didn't take long for her to learn her name. When I said those special words to her, "Tari Tari" she would perk up and wonder what I wanted. But we still had a long road ahead of us.

She had already been with me at least two months, longer than normal for me to teach a rescued dog that people are okay and that life is worth living. Then we had a setback. A silly setback. Sometime during the night I went into the bathroom. Sitting there, basically asleep, Tari Tari left her blanket in the corner of the kitchen and came to me. She asked for the first time to be picked up and held. She reared up and placed her little front paws on my leg and asked to be picked up. I did as she asked. I picked her up, held her for a moment, probably mumbled something to her and then realizing my hands were filled with dog, reached over and set her in the bathtub, beside where I dozily sat. Finishing my call of duty, I stumbled back to bed.

In the morning, I bounced out of bed, and within minutes headed back to the bathroom. Plopping myself down, I looked sideways at the bathtub. There sat Tari Tari. Cold, forgotten and once again in a situation of discomfort. Any other dog would simply have jumped out of the tub. Not Tari Tari. Her little face said it all. "You put me here. I have spent the night here. If this is what you want, then so be it."

One day Tari Tari actually fell asleep in my arms. It took months and months for her to relax enough to quit panting in fear, let alone fall asleep in my arms when I was holding her. She began to love for me to pick her up and hold her. But it always had to be on her terms. First she would allow it by giving me what I had grown to call her growl bark—a sound she reserved only for me. I had to let her wrap her front legs around my arm as I picked her up. Once up, she had to throw herself over my right shoulder and cling to me like she was drowning. She would keep a rigid and trembling posture. She would often go, even willingly, to my friends and acquaintances and stand upright, and for a split second even place her front paws on their leg. But they could never reach down and pick her up for it scared the heck out of her, and her not so good little heart would race madly and she would pant excessively until released. Eventually, in good weather conditions, Tari Tari actually went outside and played with spiders and grasshoppers. As far as housebreaking, she learnt not to soil inside. She learnt how to play and communicate with the other dogs much like a seven- to twelve-week-old pup learns these skills. She formed an incredibly firm bond with me as long as I remembered that she was not an ordinary, properly raised dog. She did not stick by my side like most of my other dogs but whenever I looked at her, she always seemed to be looking back at me.

She came to know the warmth and comfort of a house where all little lap dogs belong, to know her name and most importantly, to know love.

RUN FOX RUN

As I hadn't taken my house pack for a daily run early in the day, they were starting to hound me unmercifully. There was no way they were going to let me relax and watch the evening six o'clock news. Half a dozen were all trying to fit in my lap at the same time. This, of course, meant snapping and snarling at each other as they fought to keep a couple of inches of space to themselves. One of my little girls kept running back and forth between me and the dog door leading outside. Clearly she was tired of waiting for me to head out with her and the others for a run out in the horse pasture. She finally convinced me I was shirking my responsibility by picking a fight with another dog right in front of the television.

Muttering to myself about the dogs who were my boss instead of the other way around, I stomped outside. The only way to get them to quit scrapping was going to be with a long walk. Because even with total freedom just on the other side of the dog door, there was no way they would go by themselves.

As I weaved back and forth all over the open grassland of the pasture, furry bullets pinged past me running and playing. Whenever some of them realized they were quite a ways from me, they would literally swap ends in mid-stride and come hurtling back towards me. My, they were having fun. I couldn't help but smile at their absolute joy over their choice of exercise. Strolling along, I headed towards the yard, with the intentions of zig-zagging through a stand of poplar and willows. Back at the house, my outside dogs who are penned when the inside dogs are free, set up a howling chorus of frenzied barking. Something they had been doing every night after dark for two solid weeks. Time and time again I had gotten dressed and went out with the flashlight to try and spot what was setting them off.

Pausing just inside the edge of the trees, I stared in amazement at the fox near the dog pen. The nervy fellow, still in good daylight, without a care or worry over the howling dogs, lifted his leg and left his mark on the corner post of their pen, inches from their drooling jaws. The nerve.

About then, Casey, one of my Jack Russels caught up with me. Jack Russels are born and bred in the United Kingdom to hunt down and even kill fox. Casey, who had never hunted a creature in her sheltered life, spotted the fox and her hackles shot straight up on her neck, all the way down to her stubby tail. She headed for the fox flat out, low to the ground. Real low to the ground as a matter of fact. As she was only a few days from her due date, her pregnant belly must have been brushing the ground. The fox leapt sideways and lit out for the thick row of Saskatoon bushes bordering the ditch and the road. Casey never stood a chance of catching that fox and he knew it. Zip, he was through the hedge. Having lost sight of him, Casey came panting back to me. Glad Casey had given up the chase in her condition, I gave her a pat and turned around to call the rest of the dogs to me. The fox had simply run down the ditch on the other side of the thick bushes and emerged back on a horse path less than two hundred feet from me.

Although he never looked at me, I know he was well aware of my presence. A bold, strikingly beautiful creature in his prime, he must have known I was not a human to be feared. That was all well and fine for him, but his size was two to four times greater than some of my house mutts, which made me nervous that he may take a nip out of one of their curly hides.

Bailey spotted him next. She gave a tremendous howl, and quicker than Jack Flash, was in full stride. Not after the fox mind you, but straight at me. Her Poodle body hit me hard enough in the chest when she leapt into my arms from the ground to almost knock the wind out of me. Knowing something horrible was out there in the trees and going to eat them alive, the rest of my pack came racing to me, their protector. Some pressed themselves against my legs, while others headed for the safety of the yard, all screaming. All but one.

One brave, coal-black, mighty hunter named Rockin Ronnie, was the toughest, greatest, Shih-tzu ever. Rockin Ronnie lived her life with me because I couldn't find a perfect home for her because she was a confirmed cat killer. Once that pushed in face, chock full of needle sharp teeth came in contact with a poor cat, it soon ceased to exist. Her battle scars showed through on her lips, ears and body. The main reason cats fell prey to her was because, like my Polly dog, both of them hunted like cats themselves. With stealth, slow and steady. With patient determination. Cats were just too used to normal dogs and generally could escape them.

Without a sound, like any brave dog, she threw herself into full chase. Just like any dog I ever witnessed, she never stood a chance of catching the fox. He taunted her. Staying just out of her reach. Gracefully toying with her. Suddenly, she slid to a stop. Slowly she sank to the ground. Now motionless, she laid facing the fox. Patiently she remained motionless. Not a muscle quivered. The fox danced around her. Twice he darted in and pretended he was going to slap her with his paw, then quickly leaping high and away. Not a muscle moved in that solid pint-sized dog.

The fox darted in and took a quick sniff of her rear end. No reaction from Rockin Ronnie. Swiftly he cleared her with a gliding leap, actually poking the back of her neck with his pointed muzzle on the way over. A motionless statue. Then he made his mistake. He came to a complete stop in front of her. Just for a second he was still. That second was all she needed. She launched herself straight at him, like a cat's final pounce on the unsuspecting mouse. Her teeth connected with the ruff of thick fur on his neck. Her teeth embedded in that fur and perhaps some hide under it. She held on as he twisted and struggled to escape. Three times larger than her, he took off dragging her along. I could see her trying to bring him down by using her powerful neck muscles to try and shake him to death. With him in full flight and her legs not even touching the ground, she couldn't have been causing him any distress at all. He lost her at a hole in the same Saskatoon bush hedge where he had lost Casey the first time. I think their bodies simply didn't fit through that hole and she was literally brushed off him.

You would have sworn though, that this mighty hunter had really done away with the fox the way she pranced back to me, her lip curled in triumph. Her short, bowed legs taking each step with pride. Her chest jutted out in glory. Way to go, Rockin Ronnie.

HOMING INSTINCT

Dogs and cats, if lost, stolen, or in any way removed from their homes, will attempt to return there once given the chance. I feel that in most cases it is the male dog who, being the most territorial, will try the hardest to return. Chico, my male Blue Heeler, made the journey home against all odds. I had, for a long time, rented a farm in the Drumheller vicinity. This was home to my herd of horses and Chico. When employment forced me to move, Chico and the horses had to remain behind until I could find an acreage to rent in my new location. Because of long work hours, and the long drive back to Drumheller, I could only return every three or four days to check on my animals. Chico always met me in the driveway, leaping and twisting in sheer delight at my homecoming. He stayed tight against me as I checked the pastured horses for any cuts, nicks or bruises. Then we would spend an hour or two playing Frisbee and games of tag. But the second I headed for the barn to replenish his tubs of dry dog food and fresh water, the poor little guy knew that in short order I would be leaving him again. Chico would then ignore me, keeping his face turned away from me in despair. As I returned to my truck for the lonesome drive home, he would lie in the barn doorway, staring off in the opposite direction, refusing to look at me. He made me feel lower than a snake in the grass.

Finally, I found a country home, finally my animals could be with me again. Chico made the journey to his new home with a smile on his face a mile wide. He radiated pure happiness.

Our troubles were just beginning. On the Drumheller farm there were no close neighbours and he never left the property. While he was forced to stay there alone, people who drove by the place told me that he often lay in the driveway waiting for my return. The new acreage was a whole new ball game. My neighbours were a few yards across the fence line. My neighbours also had several dogs. Several female dogs in fact. Chico considered himself in dog heaven. Those females were not spayed and he was not neutered.

With me gone to work sometimes over twelve hours a day, Chico needed to be contained as the neighbours told me flat out that he would receive a bullet as a wedding present the next time he got married to one of their females. I could not leave him in the house because he would destroy it. I could not leave him in the garage because the people I was renting from had a large amount of their own personal possessions stored there. I could not leave him tied in the yard either because another close neighbour had a large brute of a mongrel dog who could show up and savagely attack the smaller Chico, who would have no way to escape.

Chico had been at his new home less than two weeks and I felt, regardless of my love for him, I had no choice but to find someone else to become his master. Blue Heelers were still a fairly new breed to a lot of people in Canada at that time and within a day of making my decision, I watched his new owner drive away with Chico crouched and trembling on the seat beside him.

I had warned the man that Chico was very devoted to me and it was best if he kept him tied for quite some time to prevent him from running away and attempting to return to me.

I was to find out after that the man kept Chico only a few days. Not only would Chico not eat or even lap water, he snarled and snapped at the man every time he tried to pet him. Disgusted with the dog's attitude, he gave him away to another person living many, many miles away. If only he would have phoned me, I would have taken Chico back and tried again to find a suitable home for him. The second man kept him chained. He too, must have been ticked over the dog's behaviour. If only they would have understood that Chico needed time to adjust to them as his new masters. He needed time to not think of them as strangers who had no business touching him or keeping him tied so he couldn't come find me.

While uptown shopping a few days later, I ran into the man whom I had given Chico to. When I inquired about the dog, he said that he had given him away and just that morning heard from the new owner. Chico had snapped at him once too often and he had been in the process of "kicking the living shit out of him" when the dog had managed in his struggles to slip the collar over his head and make a dash for freedom.

My heart in my throat, tears building behind my eyes, I walked away. My little devoted dog was out there somewhere. Hungry, lost and obviously beaten. What had I done to him? Poor Chico.

I knew my dog. I knew he would try to find me, to return home. But which home? The one here where we had lived less than two weeks? Or the farm down near Drumheller where he had lived most of his life with me and would have only happy memories? I headed for Drumheller. The place was as I had left it. Empty with no signs of Chico anywhere. I visited all my old neighbours and begged them to keep a watch for him whenever they drove by the place and to phone me collect should they spot him. Just in case, I put out dog food and water in the alley of the old barn where he would be sure to find it. Back at my new home, I waited. Weeks went by and no dog. I knew the perils of a lost, stray dog. Country people do not take kindly to stray dogs hanging around. Especially ones who would not be friendly to their gestures of human friendliness. More than likely he had been shot when entering someone's property looking for food and shelter. Or hit by a car. Or killed by a pack of coyotes. I gave up putting ads in the local papers. I gave up putting it over the radio. He was gone, period.

Arriving home in the black darkness of an autumn night, tired from work, I made my way down to the stack of hay bales to feed the horses. Feeling around for the strings on the first bale, I grabbed it and yanked it from the stack. Turning, I felt something brush my leg. Fearing the unknown, I immediately dropped the bale. The falling bale resulted in a yelp of pain. Standing, half-paralyzed with fear, I watched an animal drag itself around the corner of the stack of hay. My God, it was Chico! Talking quietly to him, I gathered him in my arms and carried him to the house.

There in the bright light I looked down at the ruined creature I had placed on the hallway floor. There laid my little dog, starved to a rack of brittle bones with his dry fur falling out in places and his hind legs splayed out at a dreadful angle. His eyes turned up at me begging for kindness, his tail beating a faint hello.

Phoning the vet's emergency after hours number, I gathered him up once again, placed him gently on the truck seat and headed for town. I was expecting the vet to advise me to have the crippled dog put to sleep. I felt the fool for entrusting his life to a stranger. But after a careful and kind examination, the vet felt that Chico had probably been hit by a car and that the dog's wounds would heal enough for him to regain good use of his hind quarters. Mostly he needed the best of food and shelter. Although it didn't happen overnight, Chico did indeed heal. He remained locked in my bedroom, while I was at work, until the day he felt good enough to eat my bedspread. From then on, he went everywhere with me. He was content to wait patiently at the back door of my place of employment, curled on his blanket in good weather, under my truck in the rain or in my truck in cold times. He never wandered, he just waited, afraid of losing me again. He never again snarled or snapped at anyone, secure in his position as my dog. He was faithful and devoted until the end.

Not I, nor anyone else, will ever know all the hardships he must have endured—whether he had any food, how he became so seriously injured or how much pain he must have suffered. How in the world did he find his way back to me? He came back to a place where he hadn't lived at long enough to even establish it as his home. For Chico it must have been a journey of blind faith with a touch of miracle thrown in.

EUTHANASIA

Death is not something we like to talk about. If a person close to us passes away, friends and family understand our pain and try to be there for us. Often, though, when we lose an animal, other people can't understand our grief and offer very little heart-felt sympathy. I have found with not only myself but other animal lovers, the passing of their beloved pet causes great despair, much like the loss of a human loved one. So, let's be there in a person's time of need, even if it was only old Bowser or Queenie or Pal. I believe that the most respected veterinarian in the world is perhaps, not always the best healer, but the one who takes time to recognize the pain of the owner when they lose their pet. A kind word, a touch on the shoulder, a moment to understand the flood of uncontrolled tears, makes for a good vet. These are the doctors who will be most recommended to others when all is said and done.

I also know that, many times, euthanasia should have taken place long before it did. Many times, because of our love for a pet and perhaps a fear of death, the animal suffers much too long. Sometimes we put off the inevitable because we are selfish and do not want to go through the pain of losing our beloved pet. At these times we are not thinking of the animal's suffering but of our own. I have been there and done that. We must come to grips with our impending grief and do what is best for the creature who cannot make the decision on its own.

Perhaps the animal is not, in any way, suffering. This is another matter entirely. The list of reasons for disposing of an animal is long. I think over the years I have heard some of the stupidest reasons. Not wanting to spend the money to spay a female dog, some people will choose to drown the new-born puppies or smash their heads in with a hammer. Some people will raise a couple of litters a year and give them away and if nobody wants them, they will take them to the animal shelter where they will be disposed of. Some people decide to abandon unwanted dogs out in the country. Perhaps these people assume that country people will look after them for the rest of their lives if they don't starve to death where left. Perhaps they don't consider that wild animals could kill them. These things happen all the time and I am sick of these ignorant attitudes.

People often call me up asking to buy a pup. Some proceed to tell me that they have had lots of dogs. When I ask what happened to their pets, they tell me, "Oh, I had this one or that one put to sleep because it kept peeing on the floor" or "it bit my son" who was probably picking on it yet again or "I sure hope your seven-week-old puppies are already housetrained and won't pee on my floor." One lady informed me that she had purchased three dogs in the last three years but they all got too big so she had them disposed of. She had the nerve to ask me if my puppies for sale were going to be teeny-weeny?

A man called asking to buy a hyper, go, go, go Jack Russel puppy. He wanted to know if it would be happy living in the garage all the time as the last Toy Pomeranian went nuts locked up in the garage without ever being let out. The same thing happened to the tiny Poodle he tried to keep there before that.

I ran into another lady on Main Street and asked her how the little dog she had purchased from me was doing. She said she had it put to sleep because its fur got too matted and she didn't want to take it to a groomer all the time. When I sold her the pup, I told her that a Poodle had to be groomed on a regular basis. She said, of course, she knew that. The icing on the cake was when she said the kids were hollering for another dog and she would drop by when she had the time to buy them another one. I don't think so, lady.

The majority of my calls from people looking to purchase a pup start out the same way. "My kids are after me for a pup, what do you have to make my kids happy?" I know that most dog breeders readily sell these people a pup. I don't until I make sure the parents really do want a dog in the house and aren't just buying the pup to please the kids. Chances are, when the kids get over the original glee of owning a dog, they no longer have time for it. So the adult must feed it, clean up after it and pay the bills for owning it. Pretty soon the dog is nothing but a pest to have around. The dog ends up sold, given away, taken to the SPCA or put to sleep.

In my life I have had to dispose of sick, dying or injured cattle, horses, cats and dogs. I know how to do it quickly, properly and painlessly. It is never a pleasant task, especially if it is one of my own cherished pets. I always feel such an emptiness inside me afterwards. Life does not seem fair, but I will not allow an animal to suffer needlessly.

I can also be very abrupt with people when I see them allowing their animals to suffer. I once came upon a dog in terrible despair. For many days, his entire mouth and face had been full of porcupine quills. In dismay, I asked why nothing had been done for the starving, suffering dog. Well, it seems, they didn't like the dog, in fact, really disliked him because he had killed their precious kitty cat. So he could just suffer for what he had done.

Now for the worst thing I ever saw. It makes me want to vomit, even now, just putting it down on paper. I went to another man's home to look at horse hay that was for sale. There in the yard laid a grand old dog. Unable to even raise his head, nothing more than hide covering his bones. At first I thought he had been dead for quite some time and his body simply hadn't been disposed of. Then he whined. I almost fainted realizing that the dog was still alive. Approaching the body, I could smell nothing but rot and decay. Kneeling down, I went to touch him. The man said, "don't bother him, he is dying."

The tears already starting to fall, I choked out, "why?" The man proceeded to tell me that he and his family loved that old dog with all their hearts. They had had him many a year. Now, rotting with cancer, he was dying. He hoped the end would come soon.

The dog was lying in the hot sun, unable to drink a mouthful of water even if the empty dish twenty feet away could offer him a drop. Standing up, I offered to do the humane thing for him and put the old dog out of his misery.

The man looked me square in the eye and told me that apparently I wasn't an animal lover. He suggested that I had never loved an animal or I would not be able to suggest such a cruel thing and told me that the dog would die when he was ready. He could not understand that putting a beloved animal out of its pain and misery was kind.

As you might be able to guess, I never fed that man's pocket book by buying any horse hay from him that day. What I did do, was suffer days without sleep, my heart shredded, thinking of that faithful human companion who laid dying without anyone who cared enough to end his suffering.

SKUNKED

I was fast asleep behind my closed bedroom door with the portion of my pack who are privileged enough to sleep with me, when I was rudely awakened. Skunk. The odour was drifting under the door, making my sleeping beauties snuffle and snort right along with me. Man, oh man, was the horrid stink ever strong. My first fear was that a silly skunk had wandered right into the house through the dog door. Then I realized that couldn't have happened because the other dogs would be going nuts in the kitchen if a skunk had really come into their home. Not taking any chances though, I slowly opened the door and took a peek. Now the smell really hit me. The only black-and-white creature out there was one of the dogs. Stepping careful, I came into the kitchen where two of the dogs were frantically rubbing their faces all over the kitchen floor in an attempt to get the stink off themselves. Gagging, I went into motion and called a nearby friend to pretty please come and help hold the two stinkers while I used Odour Mute to neutralize the smell. We used the whole bottle before we were finally able to draw a breath of semi normal air. Then I set to scrubbing the floor where they had rubbed some of the skunk spray off themselves.

Something was still really wrong with the whole scenario though. The smell still seemed to be particularly strong over by the stove. There sat my Cockapoo, Racey, seemingly unconcerned with what was happening. I should have known that if any dogs were out hunting in the dark, Racey would be one of them. A couple of steps in her direction confirmed my fears.

Now what to do? The Odour Mute was all gone and I didn't have a single drop of tomato juice in the whole house. My friend was kind enough to volunteer to head for town to the only store open twenty-four hours a day. Off he went on his mercy mission.

He told me that the second he entered the convenience store, the staff started to cross their eyes and whisper about him. On seeing him carrying every single little can of tomato juice they had on the shelf, surely they must have figured out that maybe he had been in contact with a skunk.

We ended up soaking Racey in the tub with the juice, rubbing it well into her fur and then giving her a good rinse job. She remained faintly smelly and more than faintly red in colour.

My poor house had the smell embedded in the walls, the curtains, the floor...everywhere. My friend thought he would be a wise man and bought me a dozen car air fresheners to put up all over the kitchen. My house then smelled like the inside of a car that had just ran over a skunk. Pee-ouu!

PANDY'S ORPHANS

The loss of my dog Pepper left me with five three-day-old orphan puppies. They laid curled in sleep, woven together like balls of soft yarn, unaware that their mother had just died a horrible death when the stitches from her caesarean gave way. My dear friend, Simone, took the gruesome task of cleaning up the blood spattered floor, while I fought to see through my tears and placed Pepper's still warm body in a suitable box for burial. Looking at her lying in that box with her torn body already staining the new white sheet I had lined the box with, totally destroyed me. As if I were a small, helpless child, Simone comforted me, until I was able to come to my senses. My busy schedule would not allow me to care and feed these wee orphans every two hours, night and day. Dialling my friend Pandy's phone number, I prayed she would be home. When she answered, I again lost control, sobbing, I told her of the death of my charming, tail-wagging Pepper.

Within minutes Pandy and Len were at my house. I explained that the task of raising these new-borns would take up every hour of their lives, at least for the first while. Their quiet, tranquil life would abruptly come to an end. Neither Len, nor Pandy, so much as blinked an eye. They simply showed how wonderful a couple they were and set to learning the how to and how not to feed, clean and care for the now hungry and crying little ones. This then, is Pandy's story.

With only a crash course in the feeding and care of the five soft as silk puppies, we headed home to town, loaded with formula, feeding syringes, baby bottles, cotton balls, extra blankets and wash cloths. And of course the orphans, tucked warmly into a towel-lined, insulated food hamper, just right for a cozy puppy nest. Having raised two sons, I figured I knew a lot about midnight feedings and diaper changes. In the next seven weeks, those girl puppies were going to show me that, yes, I knew about human babies, but boy did I have a lot to learn about puppies. Already we were the proud owners of two other dogs. Huge, gentle and loyal are the only words to describe our crossbred male dog Leo. We also had Miracle, a petite Poodle pup, white as driven snow and unfortunately, destined to a short life of illness. And now, we had the Quint Sisters. To start with, I found it helpful to simply call them, girl puppies one, two, three, four and five.

For the first six days, I religiously fed the girls every two hours, morning, noon and all night. Gradually I was able to increase the time between feedings to three hours, then finally four hours. At first I tried using the doll-like baby bottles that Gayle had given me, but the hungry little ones sucked the formula so fast, they literally had milk going into their mouths and pouring out their noses as they couldn't swallow fast enough. So I switched to syringes (no needle attached) and in this way could control how fast they ate.

Now for the other main part of raising orphan puppies! A mother dog licks and cleans her puppies to get them to void their bowels and bladders. I had to find a way to stimulate these body functions after feeding in a way similar to a mother dog's tongue. At first I used dampened cotton balls. Too slow and frustrating. I finally settled for slightly moist face cloths. Not for human use again I might add.

I mixed fresh formula, not too hot or too cold, for each feeding. Afterwards, I sterilized all the feeding equipment so it was ready for the next feeding. The total time spent per feeding would be a good hour from start to finish. As you might guess, I was quite short of sleep before their eyes finally opened at about two weeks old when I could spread their feeding times out even more. Soon I had them on gruel, eating and lapping from a shallow dish. What a mess my quints could make walking through their food, sitting in it and smearing it all over each other. Now I had to clean the whole pup, not just its bottom after each feeding.

Miracle, on her good days, loved to get in with the quints and teach them to play. She was about five months old and already the pups seemed to be almost as big as her.

Gayle thought they were pot-bellied balls of scruff. I thought they were all special. I didn't want to fall in love with them because I knew that at seven or eight weeks of age they would be going to new homes, but I knew I was fighting a losing battle. They were so sweet and I was their momma. They rarely let me out of their sight, racing after me from room to room as I tried to do my housework.

Leo, at almost a hundred pounds of lumbering dog, was scared to death of them. The second he saw the pack of them racing towards him, he sprang for the door, begging to go outside. Sometimes the Quint Sisters would corner him and he would let a deep woof out at them. Instantly they would drop to the floor, turn and slink away. Not for long though, for soon they would turn around and like a miniature army, yipping their war cries, they would head straight for Leo again. Len and I had many a happy laugh watching this display of puppy pack versus giant coward.

Four girls soon found new homes. Pup number five, now named Sassy stayed. She is a joy to us, bouncing up and down with the simple happiness of being alive. She thinks she is human and perhaps in my eyes she is.

TRAPPED

Hauling truckloads of hay is an ongoing occurrence around here. Horses eat as if starvation is lurking just around the corner.

I had hired two young fellows to bring in some loads of square bales from the neighbours' field. With two pickup trucks on the go, I planned to be finished in a couple of hours or so. The first load was already stacked in the back of the shed. The second load was being hurled, bale after bale, from the back of the truck by one of the boys with great enthusiasm, as only teenagers can do. The other boy swiftly stacked them in a square, high stack.

Seeing as how I was the boss lady, my job was a lot less strenuous. It consisted mainly of making sure that the rapidly expanding stack of eighty-pound bales were being packed neat and tight. The second truckload was soon in place. Then things started to go wrong.

With the trucks coming and going, I had locked up all the dogs except Jack and Jennie, my two Jack Russel Terriers. Surely I could keep my eyes on two dogs so they came to no harm. Apparently not.

Jackie Jack, the male, never sits still for a single second. On this particular day, he finally decided to lay down and take a breather, right in front of the rear tire. Even as the boy was throwing the truck into gear, I was hollering, "Whoa, stop, don't go!" Thank heavens the truck box was already unloaded because that tire ran over Jack's body like running over a lump of dirt.

Jack never made a sound, never cried out, nothing. But he was injured and bad. He tried to stand but collapsed immediately. Fully conscious, he looked up at me, his stubby tail wagging frantically.

Gently, I gathered him into my arms and placed him on my truck seat. The boy who had run him over was beside himself with despair. I patted his shoulder and told him it was my fault, not his. It was my mistake for not being more observant as to the whereabouts of Jack and Jennie when he started the truck up. Telling the boys to keep hauling loads of hay, I headed for Dr. P.'s.

The kindly vet examined Jack. Because the truck was not loaded with all the extra weight and because Jack was solid steel muscle, he felt that Jack might be mostly just sore and badly bruised. A small dog in poorer physical condition would surely be dead. Leaving the dog at the vet clinic so the doctor could care for him, I headed home.

The boys had finished bringing in the last one hundred bales and had stacked them tight in the shed, wall to wall and right to the ceiling. I went back to work out in the horse corrals, trying not to worry about Jack and hoping the tough little Terrier would be okay. Besides, I had my Polly dog to worry about too. I hadn't seen her since early morning when I had watched her heading out across the pasture, nose to the ground, hunting for her catch of the day. She should have been back by now. Most of her hunting was done at night. Her daytime trips were shorter because of the hot afternoon sun and laying in the shade was preferable to trucking all over the country.

By evening, I knew Jack would be okay. Dr. P. had telephoned to say that Jack could probably come home the next day. As for my Polly dog, she was still on the missing list. Chatting with one of the boys' fathers, he said that while I was gone to the vet clinic he had dropped over to see how the young fellows were doing. He remembered seeing Polly out in the yard while he was at my place. So she had been close to home then. I started calling for her and searching the corrals and under the out-buildings for her. No Polly.

Now call me strange if you like, but I have always had some sort of sixth sense when it concerns my most beloved pets. And my sixth sense was kicking into overdrive. It was telling me that Polly was close by and needed me now. A tight feeling in my chest was getting stronger by the minute. Starting to panic, I phoned my dear friends, Bob and Ann. The three of us searched frantically for her. It was Ann who heard the faint noise. She tried to explain to me the sound that was coming from inside the shed of newly stacked hay. She said it sounded as if a mouse or something was scratching on cement. Standing motionless, I listened as hard as possible. Sure enough I finally heard the scratching sound myself.

My friends must of thought I had lost my mind when I began throwing bale after bale, left and right, out the shed door. But they were soon by my side demolishing that stack of hay. That shed had a cement floor and that sound had to be Polly trapped somehow in the stack.

We found her squashed tight between two bales. As the last bale was hurled aside, she drew a breath of much needed fresh air and weakly tottered out of the shed to gulp down water from the dog dish on the lawn.

Able to scratch with one front paw on the cement floor, she had been saved by the miracle of Ann hearing the faint sound. The boys had missed seeing her enter the shed. Working steadily, they would have been unaware that the little dog was quickly imprisoned by tonnes of hay. It would have been the dead of winter by the time I had fed those bales to the horses, and finally I would have found her skeleton—all that would have been left of her.

TRIXIE POO

A silver-grey Teacup Poodle. She was a beauty to behold with round, shoe-button eyes, a delicate muzzle and a thick, wavy coat. She was also, no doubt, the dog most disliked by my friends that I have ever owned.

I answered an ad in the city newspaper for a year-and-a-half-old female Toy Poodle that was for sale. A couple days later, I pulled up in front of a beautiful house, a mansion in my eyes. Simply huge and surrounded by manicured lawns with winding cobblestone paths leading here and there. The lady of the house answered the doorbell, regal and dressed to the nines. She made me feel a tad bit inferior, I must say, in my ratty cowgirl jeans and scuffed boots. She gave me the once over and in a rather bored voice asked what it was that I wanted. I explained that I was the woman coming to look at buying a Toy Poodle.

Stiffly she turned around and called in the sweetest voice possible. "Trixie Poo, oh Trixie Poo, come here my baby. Someone here to visit you, Trixie Poo." Four tiny feet sinking into the thick, plush carpet brought the cutest five-pound silver dog strolling up to us. Carefully the woman reached down and ever so gently lifted the dog up into her arms. Only later was I to learn why she did it so carefully.

Eye to eye, that dog and I looked at each other. I was smitten and falling in love with her at first sight. Apparently she didn't feel the same about me because she curled her lips to reveal rather good-sized fangs for such a tiny creature. A low growl rumbled from her throat. Convinced since childhood that all animals love or will learn to love me, I told the woman that I would buy her, even though the midget's growl had become a steady snarl by now. The woman seemed pleased to hear me say that, seems everyone else that had come to look at her was put off by the dog's attitude. Not me though, brave soul that I am.

I was informed that Trixie Poo did not eat dog food. Instead I must cook for her, three meals a day. She handed me some of Trixie's favourite recipes to get me off on the right foot. Then she began to go through Trixie's wee suitcase full of clothes, explaining each item to me. An embroidered leash matched a spring doggy coat, etc. I was told that Trixie must not go outside without the proper coat on or she will get upset. Also, Trixie must be walked only so far and for so long or she will get upset. Then she must have a wee bit of lunch upon returning to the house or she will get upset. I was starting to worry that maybe I was buying someone's spoiled rich kid, instead of a cute Toy Poodle. I paid for the dog, and the woman gingerly placed her in my arms, seeming to pull her hands back fairly quickly after doing so. You would have thought, that cute dog might go to biting or something. My new pal and I headed the old Ford pickup truck for home. She laid sedately on her half of the seat for the entire journey. She only looked at me once or twice to give me a real nice "I'm pleased to meet you" snarl. Boy was I a happy camper with my new purchase. Yes siree, I had bought myself a real dandy.

Parking the truck in front of my house, I hoped Miss Trixie wouldn't mind living there seeing that it's not really a fancy mansion and it's short of fancy sidewalks and trimmed lawns. Opening my door, I asked her politely if she would like a hand down off the truck seat. She ambled over, peered down at the ground, decided that yes, it appeared to be a bit far to jump. She allowed me to pick her up and carry her to the grass and to set her down. That's when things got interesting.

Not only had I forgot to dress her appropriately, I didn't have a short leash on her either. For the first time in her life, she was free. Free. She leapt in the air and rolled in the grass. She didn't have to walk at a human pace, she could run. She zigged and she zagged. And she discovered a pile of dog food! Horrible, yucky dog food that dogs were forced to eat. She sat down and devoured the whole pile. Seeming to smile between every jaw crunching bite. Happy, exhausted and fed, she marched over to me and actually wagged her tail. A perfectly groomed tail that I suspected hadn't been wagged very often in the past. Trixie was home to stay.

I fell in love with her and she with me. Except something wasn't quite right. I was not her master, but she instead was mine. To this very day, she has me jumping on command, her every wish is my desire. Except for the dozen times she has seriously bitten me, we get along fine. One must be very careful when picking her up if she is in an off mood or you may get bitten. Don't disturb her if she is eating or sleeping or you may get bitten. Don't for Pete's sake think you are going to give her heck for anything or you definitely will get bitten. Do I think this dog is bad tempered hereditarily? That it is in her bloodlines? No, I don't. Trixie Poo is bad tempered because her first humans made her that way. By spoiling her rotten. And me? Well, I find it's easier to just keep spoiling her than battle it out with her. Besides, I think I would lose the battle.

COWDOGS, I DON'T THINK SO

When the two- to three-week-old heifer calf arrived at my place, she was a pathetic, weak little creature. Deprived of a momma and nourishment for over a week, only her fighting spirit had kept her alive.

She was a late summer calf that wasn't supposed to happen. Her mother and pasture mates were being fattened on grass before their final trip to the slaughterhouse. None of them were thought to be pregnant. As the pasture was getting poor, they had been rounded up early and shipped to a feedlot, their freedom over. No doubt at the time of the move, this tiny newborn had been well hidden in the bush by her Momma and got left behind. It was a week before the rancher spotted the starving little one drinking muddy slough water to try and survive. His intentions were just to shoot the baby, as she looked too far gone to try and save. Thank heavens he stopped for morning coffee at my house on the way to do the deadly deed. Telling me about the calf was all I needed to beg him to let me catch the calf and try to save it. He thought I was nuts but said he would rope it and deliver it to me.

Pee Wee was so weak, that she hardly put up a struggle as he unloaded her from the back of his pickup truck in my corral. I carried her into a box stall and laid her on fresh, clean straw.

Starting every two hours with small amounts of prepared calf formula, it was two days before she was able to handle the full amount normally given to a calf of her age. And in those two days, she regained much of her strength and spirit. And to show her appreciation for all my hard work, she preceded to attack me with lowered head and bawling like some mad rodeo bull on the fight. At first I thought it was cute, being rammed by this pint-sized dynamo, as a mosquito bite hurt worse. By day four, she was really gaining strength and it wasn't so funny anymore. So we came to an agreement. I will rub you all over, I will feed you on schedule and in return you will quit attacking me. Once Pee Wee realized I wasn't a predator out to eat her alive, she soon welcomed my visits.

But, being a herd animal with the instinct to be with others of her own kind, Pee Wee was in a bit of a dilemma. I had no other cattle on the place. What I did have though were Dalmatians just about her size. Just about her colour too, except where she was all white, they were white with black spots. So Pee Wee became a cowdog! She went everywhere with those three dogs. And I mean everywhere. Those Dals would scoot under the bottom wire of the fences. Pee Wee right behind them. The Dals would bound up the steps, onto my deck. Pee Wee right behind them. When I opened the door into the house, the Dals would shoot by me, heading for the couch. Here is where I put my foot down. I would block her path, and push her back outside. The Dals were house-trained but by golly, Pee Wee wasn't and I suspected was never going to be. Boy, she would get mad at me for making her stay outside. I was sure glad she had no horn buds, as she thought nothing of giving me a head butt, trying to get in.

Her growth was seriously stunted from her forced starvation and she remained much smaller that a normal Charolais her age. Knowing she deserved to be with her own kind and lead a cow's life, not a dog's, I eventually sold her to my friend, Margo. It took some time for Pee Wee to take to living in a pasture with cows, and to act like a cow, not a dog. Because of her small size, she continued to duck under all Margo's fences whenever she felt like it. When she was full-grown, she produced a calf, who although born small, in a matter of four months, towered over his tiny Mom. He had to kneel to nurse by the time he was only a few weeks old. Pee Wee continued to show behavioural traits much like a dog, and in my heart remained as my one and only, true blue cowdog.

Margo, of course, had to come up with her own strange cowdog. So enter Pig into the picture. That's right, a wild boar, simply named Pig.

Margo's husband had purchased a herd of wild boar. It only took a couple of years for Margo to start disliking pigs intensely. Their habit of always getting out and rooting up her lawn so it looked like a mine field after the war, had her mumbling obscenities. So the pigs were rounded up and taken away to pig heaven. All the pigs, that is, except one part-grown girl pig.

She escaped simply by being either hidden in the haystacks or out rooting in the bush.

Now pigs are social animals who desire the company of their own kind. Well Pig's family was gone and she needed a friend. So Margo became her family. She took to following Margo everywhere. Once she tamed down, her greatest joy was being rubbed and scratched by this human who didn't like pigs. But she was slowly growing in Margo's affections. Well, maybe not always. She would get into the porch and pull down all the saddle blankets off the racks to sleep on them. She would eat all the cat and dog food as if she were starving. The only ones likely to starve were the cats and dogs because of lack of food.

If she wasn't sleeping with one of Margo's dogs, curled up together, snoozing in the early spring sunshine, she could be found curled up with the young stallion, whenever he laid down and stretched out.

Pig was sort of handy to have around too. When Margo had to pull the twines off the big round bales to feed the horses, Pig would grab the strings in her mouth and help Margo pull them off.

Pig became rather handy at helping Margo move cattle too. There the pair of them would be, rounding up the cows and calves on foot, pushing them down the road to the spring pasture. Pig, grunting and trotting back and forth, no doubt in pig language, saying "Move along there, let's go, hee hah, move em out."

Quite a pair, Margo and her cowpig. Hee Hah!

LET SLEEPING DOGS LIE

There are many reasons to let sleeping dogs lie. Take my own sleeping habits, for instance. I have the habit of wanting to roll over on the odd occasion when I'm in bed. I also have the habit of sleeping with up to a dozen or so of my canine friends. On a typical night I brush my fangs, put on my jammies and open the door to my bedroom. Like wild animals heading for their den, those cute little monsters are through the door and on the bed like they have killer hounds on their tails. With determination I push and shove my way into bed, and bury myself under the covers. Now I must spend several minutes being mauled by the little devils until they play themselves out and start finding themselves a spot to curl up for the night. Each one will end up curled tight around me. Cinnamin's preferred spot is under my chin. Trixie and her daughter, Angel, sleep under the covers, tight against my legs. Debbie lies against my upper back so she can wash my neck and ears for me for the next fifteen minutes. Sarah Lee sleeps in front of me, against my belly. Bambi and the others find whatever spot against me that's left over and stretch out. Now if I lie perfectly still, they all will soon be fast asleep with only the occasional dream induced twitch and jerk.

Already, I have the urge to stretch my legs, move my chin or, God forbid, roll over. If I do any of these things, I am disturbing my little darlings, and boy, do they complain. They whine, groan and maybe even give a growl of annoyance. They may even have to relocate from their chosen spot, causing a ruckus until they are all settled in again.

So sneaky me has devised a way to have a bit more room on the bed. Waiting patiently until everybody is in dreamland, I begin to inch my way up and out from under the covers. Slithering along like a snake shedding its skin, I manage to get up and out. On a good night, I can do this without waking up a single dog. Now walk around the bed and get back in on the other side. There I find that I have the whole side of the bed to myself. If I behave myself and don't get carried away with tossing and turning, I have lots of room and the dogs don't even miss me.

Dogs are creatures of habit. They also have buried within them, the natural instincts of their wild, untamed ancestors. Any and every dog may someday bite if woken up or annoyed while he is sleeping or resting in his chosen den. His den might be his kennel, his basket, his doghouse or even his corner of the couch. If the dog considers his resting spot his personal territory, then leave him alone when he is taking refuge there to sleep or just to get away from too much pressure in his life. An injured or frightened dog who goes to his den should be handled very carefully while attempting to remove him from it. He went there to feel safe and secure and may resent, even bite if forced to leave it. An overheated dog who seeks the shade on a blistering hot summer day should also be left alone or approached with care. He may not be thinking quite right, as he lays there panting from hard work or play. Let him have some time to cool down first.

Puppies need their sleep. If you have just brought home a cute bundle of fur, just weaned from his mother and transported to a new home, more than likely he is a bit fearful of his new surroundings. He is used to having his mother and litter mates around him. He is used to the humans who raised him and the smell and layout of the house he was born in. He may like being picked up and cuddled, but you can't seem to put him down, he's just so cute that you want to mother him. He may be used to being held and kissed, but not all day long. He may be used to being played with, but not all day long. A pup soon becomes exhausted from lack of sleep. He may even think he wants to be held all the time and try to sleep in your arms but what he needs is to be given his own den and left alone to sleep. Once sleeping peacefully, he should be left alone until he wakes up on his own and wants to socialize again. A puppy will naturally sleep several times a day, just like a human baby. You would never think of continually waking up a young baby just to play with it, so don't do it to your new puppy either. More than one new owner has caused such stress on their little furball by depriving it of adequate periods of rest, that they have ended up with a sick pup on their hands. A human being who never gets enough rest soon becomes either mentally exhausted or is prone to illness and/or injury. Puppies are no different.

I have heard of two cases where puppies were literally played with to death. Their new owners loved them to death.

They couldn't put their puppies down, they loved them so much. They couldn't stop playing with the puppies. Between each member of the family's turn with the puppies, they started getting sick and weak. Both times, extensive autopsies showed that the puppies' probable cause of death was sheer exhaustion or lack of suitable periods of rest or sleep.

BIG SISTER ANNIE

Annie came into this world as black as coal and with a high-pitched squeak like a mouse with her tail caught in a trap. The litter of tiny, furry Cockapoo puppies were pushing and shoving against their mother Mia's belly, and Annie was right in the middle of the bunch, squeaking like crazy should one of her siblings make a grab for her chosen nipple. Other than her odd new-born voice, she appeared to be no different than the rest of them. At about two weeks of age, when their eyes started to open, Annie's right eye seemed to have some sort of infection in it and remained semi-shut. I carefully doctored it each day and it finally cleared up but the tiny red bump remained in the corner of her eye. As I fully guarantee the health of each pup when selling them, I kept Annie back. By the time the eye was completely normal I couldn't bear to part with my Annie. Though sometimes I think my life would have been a lot easier without her and her ability to always be up to no good.

Long after Annie had been weaned, she still managed to find milk supplies. She would sneak slowly and quietly on her belly right up to another dog, Betsy, and her nest of young ones. Betsy always registered a look of surprise when she opened her eyes to find the black, ten-week-old pup, four times the size of her apricot babies, right in the middle of them, nursing away.

I finally had to get down right firm with Annie when she was three months old and started stealing milk from Cinnamin's new-born babies. Especially since Cinnamin, being a Teacup Toy Poodle, was herself dwarfed by the thief's size. The last time I caught Annie latched on and happily sucking away, she knew she was in trouble again when I hollered at her. She jumped up and tried to beat a hasty retreat, but she was so firmly attached to that poor mother's nipple, and just plain forgot to let go, I suppose, that there she was with an upside down Toy Poodle hanging from her chin. Mild and meek Cinnamin just hung there until her weight pulled her out of Annie's mouth and she fell back onto her blanket. How Annie got away with being a milk thief from these two mothers I can't figure out since both Betsy and Cinnamin were ferocious in keeping all other dogs and pups away from their litters of young.

If any particular one dog is to come to mind who has a dozen irritating things about it, it would have to be Annie. She takes great delight in nipping at your pant legs from behind when you are carrying heavy buckets of water or bales of hay to the horses. She manages to get my horse, Pokey, kicking at all the dogs, by jumping up and swinging from his tail. She can steal your shoe, glove or hat quicker than a fox after a chicken. She also has the world's highest yap. Now after months of telling her to pipe down, she actually does her best. She starts out, *yappity, yap, yap, yap*. I snarl at her and she suddenly develops a form of laryngitis. This does not mean that she shuts up. Instead she continues but in the strangest change of voice imaginable. Now her yipping is a combination of snorts, snuffles and snuffs done as quietly as Annie could ever do anything in her life.

When Annie was about a year old, Mia produced another batch of pups. As usual, she was a very protective mom, even I was unable to safely reach my hand in her large kennel by the kitchen stove. The other dogs were mighty careful about getting too close to the kennel. Annie was the bravest that first couple of days, squirming on her belly right to within a foot or two of the kennel before Mia's warning snarl would make her stop advancing and lie there in a position of submission.

Three days after Mia had given birth, I got up in the morning and as usual was greeted by my happy pack of dogs, bouncing around me like they hadn't seen me for over a month instead of a mere eight hours. Mia, of course, stuck her head out of the kennel, gave me a warning glare and disappeared back inside it. But wait, I was short one dog. No Annie. Figuring she was just outside, I started in on my morning chores, feeding everyone, including quickly popping Mia's breakfast into the front of her den. Still no Annie. As she had a giant appetite, I had expected her to come barrelling through the dog door from outside by now. Standing out on the steps, I shouted for her, with no response. Now I was starting to worry. I checked every room in the house without finding her. She knew better than go out to the road, but I headed there to check if she had been hit by a car. Nothing on the road or anywhere in the ditches. Next I checked the horse corrals and pasture, maybe a horse's hind hoof had finally found its mark. Still no Annie. She wasn't under any of the buildings either. I was sure no one could have stolen her in the night as Annie would not go to strangers. Next I got into the truck and drove all the roads around my acreage, hoping to find her wandering along. She wasn't at any of the closest neighbours'. It seemed that she had just plain vanished into thin air.

All afternoon I moped around, at a loss as to her whereabouts. Just before supper, I folded up a fresh blanket for Mia's kennel, and prepared myself for getting Mia safely out of her home so I could check the health of the puppies and put in a clean blanket. Talking quietly I knelt down in front of the kennel and carefully peered inside. There in the back of the kennel behind her coal black mother was my missing Annie. Four of the seven new-borns were happily nursing from their mother. The other three were desperately trying to nurse from their big sister Annie. Lovingly, Mia was licking her four and just as lovingly, Annie was licking her three. Well to say the least, I was more than a bit shocked. Annie had once again squirmed her way into a mother dog's house and home, without getting attacked. At least she was not there to steal milk but if she had any to give she would have been in seventh heaven.

Those seven pups did learn who had milk and who didn't. They had to learn because Annie would not stay out of her mother's kennel. Both their mother and their big sister raised those pups from then on. Annie was almost as protective of them as Mia was, warning the other dogs off if they came too close, responding with worry and concern should one of them cry out in distress.

As they grew and on wobbly legs began to explore, Annie guarded them from any and all dangers they might encounter. Although she had a bad habit of trying to play roughly with other waddling pups, she was as gentle as could be with her baby sisters and brothers. She would roll them over with her nose or front paw, then sit there with her head cocked on an angle, watching them turn right side up again. Should one of them squeal with annoyance at her game she would get all worried and lick and clean them until they quit crying. That's my Annie.

SPRING HAS SPRUNG

Ah, glorious morning sunshine. Feeling lazy to the bones, I found the kitchen chair Brat was laying on and sat down on the edge of it with my back to him. True to form, he immediately jumped up and stood on his hind legs scratching at my back with his front claws. Turning slightly left and right, I let him find my itchy spots and do his job as a live back scratcher. Satisfied, I moseyed over to check out Rockin Ronnie's pups.

Seeing me coming, she jumped up and hopped out of her kennel to come and say good morning. One fat, three-week-old pup remained firmly attached to her, bouncing along beneath her, suckling with fierce determination. Disconnecting him, I gave him a kiss on his wet little face and placed him back where he belonged. The next thing I saw was a cute apricot Cockapoo puppy, about seven weeks old, over by the fridge chewing hungrily on something. Whatever it was wasn't going down the hatch very easily. Scooping up the pup, I took hold of his new-found toy and extracted it from his mouth. There I stood with an annoyed pup in one hand and a dead frog in the other. Obviously, my dog Polly had found the frog somewhere on her nightly scavenging hunt. He was unlucky to come out of hibernation with the first burst of spring, probably straight into her waiting jaws. Opening the porch door to start my morning chores, I caught a faint but unmistakable odour of skunk. There sat Polly. Perhaps she had been down wind of an annoyed skunk. At least she wasn't soaked in the stinking smell. Then I noticed something at Polly's feet. Good Lord, she had managed to find a dead skunk and bring it home. On closer inspection, it was only the head of a dead skunk. I decided that I was really going to have to do something about Polly and her nightly hunting. Taking care of the remains, I headed outside.

Spring had sprung. The first shoots of grass were struggling to rear their heads up from the crumpled brown growth of last year's grass. In the distance I could hear the mallards on the big slough across the road and to the east of my acreage. They had begun returning three to four weeks before. I always feel that they bring spring with them and it is good to see them returning in the spring, ready to begin nesting and rearing their young. The horses raced towards me, kicking up their heels in the warmth of the sun. Oh, glorious spring, hello. Goodbye cold, cold winter.

I had stopped for a morning coffee and chat on the phone with my friend Barb. She soon had me laughing like a hyena over one of her escapades with her horses. Seems she had gone to the quarter of land she owns to feed her mares there. Now, Barb has a rich, gorgeous mane of black hair falling long and wavy down her back. When she bent over to crawl through the four-strand barbed wire fence, the sharp steel barbs caught and snarled tight in her hair. There she was, trapped, as good as chained to the fence. Bent over, halfway through the fence, unable to go forward or back, unable to even stand straight, unable to reach the tangle of hair behind her, unable to stand the pain of ripping her hair out by the roots to free herself she wondered if anyone would ever come along this back road to help her. Well, a man did eventually come trucking down the road and did stop to untangle her hair and free her. As she said, thank heavens he was a friend, not a foe, as she would have been at his mercy. I just pictured this episode in my mind being downright hilarious and almost choked on my coffee I was in such hysterics of merriment. Little did I know—never laugh at someone else's misfortune for you may soon have some of your own.

The chores were going well, when Bambi and Brat decided to have it out with each other, once and for all. Although Bambi, my white male Toy Poodle, outweighs Brat, my red male Toy Poodle by four or five pounds and stands two inches taller, Brat has always been top dog. Bambi considers himself a lover, not a fighter, and rarely can be bothered to even attempt to stand up to Brat. Brat is always prancing around, growling and telling all the other dogs that he is boss man on this acreage. Well, I would suppose that with spring in the air and the female dogs starting to look pretty interesting lying around in the sun, Bambi decided enough was enough with Brat and his bossy attitude.

Amazing enough, not a single drop of blood was shed in what was one of the most noisy and horrific male dog fights I have ever witnessed. Brat has always scrapped in the most abnormal position you could imagine. He fights standing upright on his hind legs, dancing around like a curly-haired miniature Boxer, waving his front paws in front of his chest.

Springing up and down, weaving left, then right, his fangs exposed between tightly curled lips with hideous snarls exploding from him, he showed his fighting spirit. Bambi, crouched like a stalking tomcat, snapping his teeth together like steel castanets, his own snarls matching Brat's. Louder and louder were their rage-filled voices. I doubt they would ever have touched each other if Brat had not stumbled and practically fell on top of Bambi. Physical contact having been made, they rolled over and over, locked in combat. By the time I had jumped the fence from the horse corral and raced over to them, the fight was over with. Neither appeared to be the victor, both slinking off in opposite directions. Expecting to have to deal with some bad bites in need of doctoring, I examined each of them from head to toe. Nothing. Not a hair out of place on either of them. All that rage and snapping jaws and not a mark. Brat did have a lot more respect for Bambi though. And Bambi seemed just a bit more cocky around Brat afterwards too. Considering that they had sounded like an entire pack of crazed wolves, they had both been more bark than bite.

With my chores done, I decided to get down on my hands and knees and clean the winter straw out of one of the insulated doghouses. When I had this doghouse built, I had specified a smaller, more narrow opening into it. Half laying on my side, I reached my arm as far inside as possible to drag the straw bedding out. If I could just get my shoulders through the doorway, I could reach the back of it. Twisting, grunting and groaning I wedged my shoulders inside. I could now reach the back and drag the straw forwards. Hey, just a second here, was I perhaps stuck? Let's see, twist a bit, turn a bit, get one shoulder out and I would be fine. I was wedged half in and half out of that narrow opening like a cork in a wine bottle. My coat had rolled up on my ample ribcage and it seemed I wasn't going anywhere. It's amazing how quick panic sets in, in a situation like this. I did fleetingly remember laughing at Barb earlier in the day over being trapped in a similar silly situation. Could the Good Lord be perhaps punishing me for laughing at someone else's folly? Would someone eventually come along and seeing my rear end protruding from a doghouse perhaps phone the rescue squad to come use the jaws of life and get me out? Would they come along today? This week? This month? My pack of friends were jumping all over me. Would one of them suddenly become Lassie and run to the neighbours' for help? Somehow I doubted it. I bet it took a good hour of squirming around before I managed to work my coat up off my sides and then my shoulders so it only remained over my head, smothering me in the close air of the doghouse. I now had the needed inch or two to work my way backwards to freedom. By the time I was out and gasping fresh, clean spring air, my devoted little buddies who I thought would give their lives for their master, had all left me to die and gone back in the house. So much for any budding Lassies in my pack.

THE DAY I LOST BAILEY

The second I opened my eyes that morning I just knew it was going to be another hectic, rip-snorting day. The neighbours' dogs had paid one of their three o'clock in the morning visits. Huge, mongrel-type critters who, by drifting into my yard in the dark, always managed to set my pack of pint-sized spitfires off like a smoke alarm. My little darlings (not what I call them at three a.m.) screeched and howled at the intruders. Stumbling out of bed, I had opened the front door and let loose with my own version of screech and howl. Good doggies that they are, the intruders turned tail and headed for home. You would never guess it though, because for at least another hour my pack continued to defend its territory without let up. Finally, they all settled back down and I had managed to get another hour or so of sleep.

Needless to say, I was more than a bit tired when I fumbled my way out of bed. I did notice that the pack intended to sleep in after doing guard duty so well during the night. Not even taking time for coffee I got to work doing the morning dog and horse chores. I had to hurry because I was scheduled to make a flying trip to Stan and Janice's to pick up some hay. Jumping into the truck, I fired the old boy up and was set to head out when I heard Bailey ricochet off the door. Dancing up and down, she stared up at me peering at her through the window. Her eyes said it all, "Can I come, Mom, huh, can I? I'll be good, Mom, honest I will, can I pretty please come with you?"

So Bailey and I headed for Stan and Janice's. Now this is one fine couple and I love visiting them. Besides growing good hay, they are super people. Best of all are their animals. Two fine farm dogs, looked after with care. The occasional friendly cat without a care in the world. Fine cattle, fat and very well cared for. On this particular morning, I had the good fortune to be taken into the calving barn and witness the most unusual new-born calf. His hair was unlike any calves' I had ever seen. Instead of fine and silky, it was dense wool. No written words could ever describe accurately his unusual, thick, frizzy coat. His colouring was as if a painter had tried to make the most perfect markings. An off black, with a perfect star exactly in the middle of his forehead. The whiteness of the star going along with a snip of white on his nose and the white bottom switch of his tail.

Stan loaded the bale for me and the old truck groaned under the weight. I closed the tailgate, we said our goodbyes, and Bailey and I headed for home. Now I bet I hadn't driven more than a mile when I hit the first big time bump. That bale shifted off the wheel wells and thumped back on the tailgate.

The tailgate, having seen better times, popped open. Not to worry, I've hauled bales before with the tailgate down. Missing my coffee by now something terrible, I resumed my speed rather quickly. Wham, I encountered the second back-country road, springtime induced, bump. The bale took another jump towards freedom. It was now sitting almost in the back of my truck, sort of on my tailgate, sort of a third of the way off my truck. Now I was in trouble.

Easing down to a stop, I told Bailey to stay put and got out to take a look. With my stomach starting to grumble about the breakfast that should have followed the coffee, I decided that if I were to drive real slow the bale would stay put the rest of the way home. Real easy, I started out. Bailey, beginning to think this was all rather boring, elected to ride on the top of the seat, curled around my neck.

We were making pretty good time at about twenty miles an hour, hugging the ditch on the right side of the highway, when I spot an RCMP officer up ahead of me, with another car pulled over. I think to myself, "Boy, I hope I don't get in trouble when I pass him with this fourteen-hundred-pound round bale hanging out over my tailgate." Then panic set in. When I got out to check the bale, I forgot to put my seat belt back on. The officer could stop me because of the stupid bale hanging out of the back of my truck and then give me a fine for having no seat belt on. Reaching for the belt, I couldn't get enough slack to do the darn thing up. The belt was trapped in the door. I opened the door, grabbed up the slack, closed the door and did up my seat belt.

I am now flustered and approximately only two hundred yards from the back end of that police cruiser. Then I realized that Bailey was no longer draped around my neck. My God, Bailey fell out of the truck when I opened the door. I hit the brakes, the bale stayed on, believe it or not, and I leaped from the truck fearing Bailey was dead because of my stupidity. Frantically, I stared back behind me, looking for her little crushed Poodle body. No body. She must have lived long enough to make it into the ditch. Lack of morning coffee made me make at least two twirls in the middle of that highway. No Bailey. I jumped back into the truck cab to back up hoping I could spot her. I totally forgot about the police officer, scant yards ahead of me. To this day, I'm positive he wasn't looking in my direction or he would have gone for his weapon thinking some crazed woman behind him had rabies for sure.

Before I could throw the old truck in reverse, something made the faintest noise behind me. Behind the truck seat, actually. Out of the cab I jumped again. Pulling the seat forward I stared down, in behind it. There laid Bailey, with the most disgusted look on her Poodle mug I've ever seen. Grabbing her, I pulled her up and out.

Counting to ten, or was it twenty, I did my seat belt up and shifted into low gear. Creeping forward, I eased by the officer and the unlucky soul who no doubt had his total concentration. I swear though, as I passed him, he gave me a "You are one nutty lady" look, before finishing writing up his traffic violation for the other guy.

Bailey, the bale and I made it the rest of the way home. And, I must admit, the rest of the day did get better.

A MANGY TRESPASSER

Mange is a terrible skin disease that robs its victims of not only their hair, but their strength and vitality. In wild canines, it eventually leads to their death. A slow wasting away leaves a once-proud and fleet-footed creature staggering on weakened limbs, its very spirit crushed. I spotted him on Monday on the way into town to pick up the mail. The coyote was only a shadow of his former self. He stood in a farmer's field, just off the highway outside of town, staring at nothing. When I pulled over and stopped my truck, I expected him to hit a high lope for the bush line like any smart coyote does, all too aware of the dangers of man. He barely turned his head and acknowledged me. I sorely wished that I had brought a twenty-two rifle with me so I could put him out of his misery. Finally, he jerkily started for the trees bordering the field, but not before I saw that his poor tail, after losing its fur, had completely frozen during the recent winter months. About the only hair left on him was in patches on his back and some on the tops of his shoulders and legs. I knew he wasn't long for this world and I prayed his misery would soon be over.

The second time I spotted him was a couple of days later. Again it was from the road, and he looked to me to be even worse off. The third time I spotted him was much too close for comfort. I only live six miles from town and he had managed to travel those six miles, right to my doorstep.

My Jack Russels, Jack and Jennie, were running about outside. The gate to their pen was wide open so Jennie could come back in whenever she wished to check on her six-week-old puppies. In fact, that was what I was doing. I was on my knees, my back to the gate, playing tug of war with the pups with an old sock.

My Jacks don't bark much, so when the pair of them came tearing across the main corral, barking like maniacs, I straightened up and glanced over my shoulder to see what they were heading for.

My heart nearly stopped. Not ten feet from me stood that mangy coyote. He was right behind me inside my Jack Russel pen. He wasn't doing anything but standing there, motionless.

Once my heart started to tick again, too fast I'm sure, my brain kicked into overdrive. Not only was this sick coyote not in any way acting normal, he had mange which could be spread to my pack of dogs, as easy as pie. The two Jacks were circling him, waiting for him to make the first move and give them a reason to attack. He was between me and the gate. Through that gate were the steps to my house and inside that house was the twenty-two rifle I desperately wanted right now.

I might have a wee bit of age on this old body, but I took two running steps and one mighty jump and cleared that coyote. I didn't saunter up those steps either. I blasted into the house, first to the bedroom for the gun, then to the next room for the bolt. Now all I had to do was remember where I put the shells. Taking a deep breath, I calmed myself down, loaded the gun and ventured back outside.

Jennie had stayed to guard her pups and Jack and the coyote were at a stand off in the middle of my stallion corral. Jack kept diving in and taking a chunk out of the coyote while my horse reared and threatened to trample both of them. I certainly couldn't risk taking a shot at him where he was. The coyote glanced at me, his eyes sunken and sad. Turning he continued to totally ignore Jack and scrunched under the bottom wire and trotted around the high slab fence and out of sight. Scooping up Jack while he stayed behind to mark his territory, I threw him into the pen with Jennie. I would have to disinfect the dogs and the pen later. I jumped into my truck to drive around and find the coyote.

He died with the first shot. His misery was over. This may sound crazy to some of you, but I think that coyote came to find me to put an end to his suffering.

UP AND OVER, EVEN UNDER

Mandy was around nine months old when she came into my life. Physically in good condition when I purchased her, Mandy's mental state was not up to par. Although not perhaps seriously abused, she was very distrustful of human contact. She shied away from my hand whenever I attempted to reach down and pet her. What was obvious was that her first owners had made the mistake of calling her to them in order to punish her for any wrong doing. Thus she learned quickly not to come when called, but instead to make a run for freedom. Although I have had this sweet-tempered dog for years, she still is very leery of coming when called.

Mandy also has a mind of her own. She also is by far the most athletic, agile dog I have come across. More so than my

Miniature Poodles, or even more than my quicker than lightening Jack Russels. A Terrier-type, standing only fourteen inches at the shoulder and built slim like a greyhound, she is a beauty. She has a steel-grey coat and a mustache that I'm fond of leaving her with when I clip her. By the time I purchased Mandy, I had developed a system that allowed me to keep several dogs without all of them having to be in the house at one time. Besides my Jack Russel pen, where Jack and Jennie were kept for the safety of my other dogs (Jack Russels are ferocious fighters, with the capability of killing other dogs several times their size) I enclosed my entire front and side lawn into two large pens. One pen is eighty feet by one hundred and twenty feet and the other one is seventy feet by eighty feet. In each pen there is heated housing for the winter and plenty of cool shade in the hot summer sun. Each pen could comfortably house up to ten dogs. Never have I placed more than seven in them.

My Jacks run free a good portion of the day and when I'm not home they are trained to stay off the road. The second I start my truck up they expect to be turned loose while the rest of the dogs are contained until my return. The two large pens of dogs run free also, as soon as the housedogs have exhausted themselves out in the pasture and corrals with me. I rotate the dogs into the house so they know I still love them. Any dog that is truly unhappy in an outside pen lives permanently in the house. It works well and I feel that because my pens all lead onto my front deck, they are not locked away and forgotten. They can see me at all times when I'm outside working, they greet all human visitors and happily enter their pens after their freedom run on command.

This was not the case with Mandy. Poorly housetrained, nervous of human visitors and skittish around me, I decided to put her into the east side pen. She simply backed up, judged the height of the gate and in a single bound, cleared it. Then I put her in the west side pen. She cleared the six-foot gate in a single bound. This pen had held Pongo and Pebbles who are five times her size. It looked like Mandy was going to remain a permanent housedog. Thankfully, she housetrained herself after a few more days.

I was already sleeping with up to eleven dogs, so she could be a housedog, but not a bedroom dog. It soon became apparent that no matter how carefully I opened the bedroom door to enter, she shot by my feet and legs, and disappeared under the bed. Okay, she could be a housedog, she could sleep under the bed, but that's all. It wasn't long before she was sleeping on the foot of the bed, every morning when I woke up. Now she gets ninety-five percent of the pillow and I get the other five, providing one of the smaller furballs doesn't get to that five percent first.

Mandy's favourite game is climbing up and down the round hay bales stacked three high, in my yard. When she isn't playing King of the Castle on the stacks, she may be balanced on top of the narrow deck railing, I guess trying to decide if she is a cat or just showing off. This sleek little dog has total freedom and total happiness, and in all these years I have never had a single bark out of her. But her very presence speaks louder than words, canine or human. She's my Mandy dog.

Mandy goes willingly to Jay Minor whenever he comes to visit. Perhaps it is because she knows in some way about the tiny Mandy dog Jay once owned. This becoming creature, also named Mandy, was three to four years old when she came to live with Jay, his brothers and sisters and parents. Jay's older brother was a paperboy who first caught a glimpse of her, a tiny Chihuahua-Terrier cross who indeed lived an unusual life. Or shall we say, she not so much lived, but existed, in her own private hell. Penned her whole life in a large back yard with dozens of rabbits these people raised to be slaughtered for meat. She was as wild as a March hare. Mandy and the rabbits built tunnels under the ramshackle buildings to hide from the light of day. The people had no feelings for Mandy, they were more than happy to tell the kids who had spotted her to catch her and take her.

It seemed to take forever, before this frightened creature quit biting out of fear when a human hand reached down to touch her. Perhaps she knew, that when a human got a hold of one of the rabbits, something bad happened, that a life was coming to an end. Slowly she, a fully mature, adult dog, had to not only learn to trust but learn that she was a dog.

Once given real dog food, such a treat to this midget canine, she stockpiled it everywhere. Jay remembers waking up rather uncomfortable, with crunchy dog food under the covers with him. Little Mandy would spend the whole night stockpiling her precious food, especially if his older brother had brought his own dog over to spend the night. She gave birth only once, to a single pup, by caesarean. This pup would never know of its mother's strange, earlier existence and would have the chance to be a normal canine.

A Mandy dog is a special dog, I wish there were more like her.

BLACKIE

Blackie is a dog with a sweet disposition and a kind eye. Seventy-five percent of the people who come here to buy a puppy, fall in love with Blackie and would pay whatever I asked in order to take her home. But Margo really owns this sleek little dog, even if I tell people that I do. Let me tell you how Blackie came into my life.

Owning horses means that I must always be on the look-out for good alfalfa hay for them—the best hay at the best price.

So, answering an ad in the paper, I headed out to a farm, many miles from home, to look at hay. I may not have bought any hay, but I did end up with the best ball of fur you ever saw. But not without a wee bit of pulse-racing, hair-raising adventure thrown in.

Herman—that's my beat up, old, Ford pick-me-up truck who is just like a Timex watch that keeps on ticking—was feeling a bit under the weather. He had coughed a time or two and so I had taken him to the best vehicle doctor in town that I could find. Seems Herman might need a new part or two to get him back on his feet. As Herman was in the vehicle hospital, I borrowed Simone's puddle-jumper car named Spot. Off Spot and I go to look at horse hay. Spot's sort of tiny, compared to Herman, but we made decent time getting to our destination.

Well, I arrived at the acreage and things don't look quite right. I thought I owned the oldest house in the whole region of northern Alberta, but apparently not. At least the windows are intact in my ole house and my lawn is covered in grass with perhaps only a few (hardly noticeable) piles of doggy doo. These buildings here are missing a lot of glass and the yard is covered in garbage. Lots and lots of foul garbage.

I sat in Spot and wondered if I really wanted to get out to knock on the door, which was sort of hanging there on its rusted hinges. I didn't have to wonder long.

The door banged open and a man sauntered towards us. The closer he got, the more my hand itched on Spot's gearshift to find reverse. Approaching us, he seemed decent enough, just not really dressed for this day and age and not actually very clean.

Then a young, black dog, with her body bent in submission, came crawling towards him. Without a thought, he delivered a kick to her ribs that sent her flying. She never made a peep but just slunk away. I had only seconds to see the sorry state she was in. But I was here to buy much-needed hay for my horses. This man said I was to follow him to where the hay was at. As he was getting into his truck (even older and more decrepit than Herman) two more men with hand rolled cigarettes hanging from their lips joined him scratching at their crotches and packing beer bottles. I felt ill at ease, but hey, I needed to buy some hay.

Spot and I followed close behind down a long, winding, back-country trail. We finally arrived at an old, unlived-in farmyard. I pulled up along side the hay for sale and watched the three rather unsavoury men get out of that pick-up truck. I left Spot's motor running and the door open. You might say I was now more than a bit ill at ease. I was a long way from nowhere with these three rough-looking strangers. And the hay was no good, maybe for starving cattle but definitely not horses.

I also had that thin black dog centred in my brain. I couldn't stop thinking about that tiny mite, who for no reason had gone flying from a kick in the ribs. I wanted that dog. I had to have that dog. I would not leave without that dog, no matter what it took. I might be scared spitless out here in the boondocks, but that dog was coming home with me.

I thanked the man for showing me the hay and told him I would think about buying it. Then I said I wanted the dog and would pay good money for it.

Taking a drag off the cigarette attached to his lip he said, "Ah, heck lady, you can have the #*%#*% dog for free. I have been meaning to shoot it since it was born, just #*%#*% haven't got around to it."

Spot and I careened out of that situation full out. I screeched to a halt in the original yard and bailed out to catch myself one starving dog. A lady, no doubt the man's better half, and a couple of sawed-off kids were there to greet me. When I explained that the man had given me the dog, one small, pre-school child said it all. "Take the #*%#*% thing, my paw has been going to shoot it since it was born." I nabbed the frightened dog and asked the child what its name was. "Ah, we called it Blackie, but the #*%#*% thing never did know its name." I was out of there.

Simone helped me that night. We de-wormed her, gave her her shots, bathed and clipped the stinking mattes from her rear-end. Blackie never moved a single muscle as we worked on her. She remained motionless, neither struggling, nor responding to our petting and stroking. I bedded her down in my laundry room, just off the kitchen. I gave her food and water and thick layers of newspaper to go to the bathroom on. She tipped her muzzle away from me, ignoring the gentle pat I gave her.

Thank God for Margo. I was getting nowhere with winning this scrawny dog over. Margo had her mares at my place to be bred to my stallion and when she had time, she helped me with all the dog and horse chores.

I was giving Blackie food, water and the necessities of life, but Margo took the time to lie down on the floor beside her and give her love. Slowly, Blackie learned that she was not going to be hurt. Ever so slowly, she learned that humans were okay. She fell in love with Margo. Now you see why she may be my dog but really belongs to Margo. Every time Margo came with her old car, Blackie knew long before I did that she was coming down the road. She twisted and twirled in happiness, because her human was just about there. It took a while for Blackie to know the sound of Margo's new truck, but she now has it down pat. The second Margo is in the door, you will find Blackie on her knee.

BIRD BRAINED

One summer a pair of adult magpies were nesting in a small stand of trees just a few yards from my lawn. The year before a pair of crows had occupied the same nest. As the nest was in fairly bad shape, the crows moved to an abandoned nest on the other side of my acreage, a nest that at least still had sides on it. Momma magpie didn't seem to mind this nest though, she decorated her new home with stray bits of twine and an empty pack of cigarettes. Two chicks had hatched in due time and the parents were kept busy seeing to their bottomless stomachs. Before I knew it, the pair were ready to test their new wing feathers and leave the nest. One chick found flying as easy as eating and was soon all over the tree tops. The other little guy wasn't quite so sure though. Perhaps he wasn't as well-developed or had some other physical problem. He refused to leave his home and caused his family untold distress as they had to continue to feed him when he should have been off catching his own supper.

At the same time, my American Cocker Spaniel, Snoopy, was busy raising her own young in a kennel out on the lawn. Normally, all my dogs give birth inside the house but Snoopy had been banished from my house after killing another mother's two-week-old pup.

The pups were safe, warm and dry in the deep straw. They were noisy little critters though, peeping and squeaking when they scrambled for their mother's milk and when Snoopy's rough tongue cleaned them. Well, magpie junior had sharp hearing and must have picked up the pups' cries while sitting in that old nest he called home.

Late spring and early summer are hectic days for me between getting mares bred and the dogs having litters of pups. My days start when the sun comes up and sometimes I'm still

half asleep when I head for the horse corrals so early. So, this one morning, I'm halfway across the yard, one eye closed and the other propped open, so to speak, when I catch the sound of a very young pup coming from the horse pasture. You can bet both my eyes flew open in a whopping big hurry. A puppy out there by itself is staring death straight in the face. If the horses don't trample it, the foxes will glide in and make a light breakfast snack out of it. I froze in the yard, holding my breath, straining to hear exactly where the pup's shrill cry had come from. Again it came, carried on the morning breeze, ever so faintly. I still couldn't pin-point even the area it was coming from. The only pup it could possibly be would be one from Snoopy's litter. Rushing to her doghouse I peered inside. I counted five pups. Exactly what was in her litter. I had some other pups in the house but older than the cry of this one I was listening to. Besides, I had already seen to their morning needs and none were missing. Again, standing still, I heard the unmistakable cry of a pup approximately two weeks old. Well, I went out and searched at least an acre of pasture, step by step, inch by inch. Nothing. Convincing myself that I had just been hearing things, I went back to work.

It was around three weeks later when I heard that lone pup cry coming from the pasture again. This time I was totally baffled. You see, that pup was not only still out there and still alive, but by the sound of it, was growing up quite nicely, sounding like a normal, healthy five-week-old pup just learning to growl and play fight with his brothers and sisters. All Snoopy's pups were right there playing in front of the kennel. The house pups were all in the house. To the best of my knowledge there was no coyote pups anywhere near my property. Even if there was a litter of fox kits near the house, the cries of kits are distinctly different than those of domesticated dogs. Should you ever get lucky enough to observe them close up, you would hear that their cries are higher pitched and sharper than a dog's. Yet seldom heard, as their momma teaches them from birth to be oh so quiet. Out to the field I go again, searching everywhere. In the grass, heck, I even found myself picking up a couple of man-sized rocks to make sure a pup wasn't hiding in a hole under one of them. You can imagine my total surprise when there I am, bent over, nose to the ground and that lone pup gave a hearty yip from the tree branches above me. It caught me so off guard that I promptly sat down, smack on my rear end in my hurry to gaze upwards into the tree. Tilting his head, I swear that young magpie gave me a wink before emitting the next drawn out puppy growl.

Magpie junior finally gained the know-how of flight and the family moved on in their travels. Not often will magpies, with their intelligence and distrust of humans, nest so close to a human residence. I will always wonder though, if that young magpie grew up and just for the fun of it, maybe taught his youngsters to mimic a young puppy's cries to fool another unsuspecting person.

Some birds are interested in something other than imitating small dogs and kittens. One lady who used to raise tiny Teacup Toy Poodles in a rustic country setting was having a real problem with someone stealing her littlest dogs. After losing four or five to the thieves, she was ready to shoot anybody who trespassed on her property. Just about the time she was setting herself up for a nervous breakdown trying to catch the thief, she discovered the pair of very fat, very contented owls in a nearby tree. Those owls either thought the diminutive dogs were fairly stupid rabbits, easy as pie to swoop down and nab, or maybe the hunting was just so much easier on the nicely mowed lawn. After managing to scare the predators permanently off her property her dogs stopped going missing.

LOOK OUT FOR THOSE TEETH

Getting bit by a dog isn't much fun. Just ask my friend Simone's stuffed gorilla toy. My charming male Poodle, Bambi, hated Simone's big furry friend. Every time I went to Simone's house Bambi and Bailey came with me. Bailey, on entering her house, immediately made a bee line for the cat's food dish, and

Bambi made a bee line for the toy propped up in the living room. Snarling with hate, he would attempt to kill the poor gorilla every time. It wasn't a game either, he meant to annihilate it.

An acquaintance of mine once owned a big coyote hound named Greg. Someone had teased this dog with the broom since a pup. He detested that broom, as the owner's mom was to soon find out. One day while visiting her daughter, she wanted to put Greg outside. He didn't want to go, so she picked up the broom to chase him out with it. She was the one who ended up outside.

There was a good-looking adult male stray hanging around near one of the horse pastures I rented. Obviously another case of irresponsible people driving out into the country and dropping off an unwanted pet. I could see this large black dog was losing weight and needed to be taken home and fed. Perhaps I could look after him until I found him a home. Finding him in the ditch digging under the thick cover of dry fall grass in desperate hopes of finding the odd mouse to catch and eat, I stopped and stepped out of my truck. I began talking softly to him. It was the first time I had been close to him and I was a bit taken back by his icy cold, yellow eyes. He seemed to stare right through me, as if I didn't quite exist. I should have left well enough alone, but no, I had to show him my open truck and pat the seat to let him know it was okay to get in and come home with me.

He got in all right but I sure never did. The second he was on the seat, he began to snarl and his hackles raised. Now what in the world had I got myself into? The truck was still running and I didn't even dare reach in and turn off the engine. Leaving him there with the door open, I started walking to the nearest neighbour's. It was a rather long walk, in uncomfortable riding boots I might add. I was sporting a couple of good-sized blisters on my heels by the time I reached the closest farmyard. The farmer agreed to come see if he could help me take possession of my truck again. I asked for some meat to lure the dog out of the cab with and he gave me a hunk of deer roast.

When we got back, the dog had done a good job of protecting my truck. Not surprisingly no one had stolen it while it sat there running with the door wide open. Pulling up, I rolled the farmer's truck window down and tossed a small piece of meat towards my open door. That black fool was still on the fight, but hunger won out. He jumped out and wolfed the food down. I tossed another piece a little further away and he followed. Then I threw the last of it as far across the ditch as possible. The second he was away from the truck, I was out of one cab and into my own quicker than lightning. I just barely got the door slammed shut when he came hurtling back. He stood on his hind legs and stared in the window at me, his lips curled. Later that day, the farmer came back and disposed of him. It was better than seeing him starve to death in the coming winter and it was certainly better than having him running loose where he was probably going to attack someone.

Some dog bites are accidental. The one I most remember was when my two female Dalmatians were viciously fighting. Without thinking I made a grab for the most aggressive one's collar. The other girl bit the ring right off my finger without so much as leaving a scratch on my hand. I had worn the ring, which was a gift from my parents on my sixteenth birthday, for more years than I care to remember. The gold band had worn so thin with time, that Pebbles' tooth severed the band.

A friend of mine told me the story of her father's German Shepherd who went everywhere with him. Seems this one evening, her dad went to the local pub for a quick beer. The dog always laid down at the entrance to the tavern to wait for his master. The man then purchased a case of beer to take home. On coming outside, he ran into a couple of friends of his and they stood there shooting the bull. He had set the case down on the sidewalk while he talked. Deciding to go back in for another quick beer, he told the dog to guard the beer for him.

One beer led to another and pretty soon he forgot all about his dog and his beer. At closing time, he wandered out the back exit of the pub. His faithful dog spent the night guarding that beer case and dutifully waiting for his master to come out. The man came for him in the morning and knew that more than one person had made a try for the beer. The ground was littered with rocks they must have thrown at the poor dog to drive him off and long sticks they must have poked him with too. Every one of those sticks had one end chewed all to pieces. No doubt the end he was being hit with.

Dogs do have terrific memories, especially of being hurt or abused and by whom. One man's uncle had a mixed breed pup who would get a kick in the ribs from a cranky old neighbour who came to visit. By the time the pup had grown into a good size dog, that cranky old neighbour had his hands full trying to avoid getting bit by that dog. His visits became fewer and fewer. Yet that dog never once in his life curled his lip at another human being, just at the man who liked to hurt him as a defenceless pup.

One of the most splendid dogs I ever knew was a white German Shepherd. An intelligent dog who simply loved to retrieve rocks thrown into a dugout pond. You could throw a rock and watch it quickly sink out of sight and the swimming dog would dive after it.

He would pick up the correct rock two-thirds of the time and, proudly carrying it in his jaws, would swim back to shore and beg for it to be thrown in again for him. Believe it or not, he did all this with only three legs.

This beauty of a dog had spent four long, torturous days held firm in a leg hold trap. To add to the torture, the cruel man who had trapped him came each day to laugh at his struggles and taunt him. When the dog's owner heard through the grapevine where his missing dog was, he drove there as fast as possible. The Shepherd cried with joy at seeing his beloved master coming for him. Gangrene had set in and in order to save his life, the local vet had to amputate the front leg right up to the shoulder bone.

This man who had so hideously tortured the dog still had the nerve to stop in at the Shepherd's home a couple of times a year. That dog hated him with such passion that he simply came unglued at the hinges at even catching the scent of him. Until the day the dog died of old age, he would try to savagely attack this man. You know, I can't blame the dog, can you?

JUST FOOLING AROUND

I don't think my friend Don entirely trusts me anymore. It could be because I can't help pulling a joke on him once in a blue moon.

Like the time he dropped over for an afternoon visit, just got seated at the kitchen table, and I passed him the midget-sized silver Poodle who was sound asleep in my arms, with the statement, "Hold Trixie as still as possible, Don, while I whip outside and feed the horses. Whatever you do, don't wake her up because she will want to get down out of your arms and for some crazy reason with this particular Poodle, the second her feet hit the floor, she will savagely bite you in the leg." Then, nasty old me, headed outside. Twenty minutes later, I stepped back in the door, to find that Don had believed every word I had told him. His face was white with the strain of holding onto that twisting, turning, squealing dog. Man can she ever perform the Hokey Pokey when she wants to get down out of a person's arms. "Don," I said. "Why don't you let that poor tiny mutt down on the floor since she wants down so bad?" His voice was barely above a squeak, "Because I don't want to get bit in the leg." "Ahh shucks, Don," I told him. "She's so old now, she doesn't have a single tooth left in her head, getting bit by her wouldn't hurt anymore than a new-born baby nibbling your finger." Ever so gently, he sat her down on the floor, and watched her trot away without making a single pass at his leg. It took him a while to realize I had only been joking around. For some reason, he retained it in his memory that I had said she had no teeth. A couple of months later, he happens to come for another visit. We were sitting around the kitchen table, playing cards and as usual Trixie is cradled in my arms. Now it just so happens she will bite at someone who pretends to be upset with me and pretends they are going to touch me when I am holding her. She is my number one protector. Don had just lost another game, and with mock anger, was going to punch me in the shoulder. Trixie gave a deep, warning growl and I told Don," don't fool around because she will bite you to protect me." "Yah right," he laughed. "As if it would hurt getting bit by a dog with no teeth." Before I could stop him, he reached over and tapped me on the arm. Wham, she had him. I think just about every tooth in her head connected with his hand. Poor Don.

Late that fall, I talked him into dog-sitting my new Toy Poodle, Ralph. He was sort of enjoying taking him for his daily walks around town. One day, my friend Simone and I went

over to Don's and brushed, bathed and clipped Ralph until he
shone. Now before going to Don's, we stopped at the Bargain
Store and bought a fuzzy, bright blue, new-born baby jumper.
The kind with a zipper starting from the legs all the way up to
the chin. Keeping my face as straight as possible, I explained to
Don, that from now on, Ralph would have to wear this jumper
on his daily walks to keep him from getting a bad cold from
being clipped of most of his hair. First I dressed Ralph to show
him how it was done, then I had Don dress the dog to show me
that he knew how to do it properly. Simone had to keep her
back turned most of the time so Don would not see her

laughing to herself at the sight of a grown man trying to put a baby suit on a Poodle. Once Ralph was dressed to my satisfaction, I put his collar and leash on so unsuspecting Don could take him for a bathroom break. Don was starting to get a bit worried about what people would say when they saw the funny looking dog. I explained that he shouldn't let other people's laughter bother him and shooed him out the door.

I waited until Don and dog were well on their way before hollering to Don to remember to always unzip the zipper when Ralph stopped to lift his leg. His eyes got a large, horrified expression at the thought of trying to get that zipper undone in time for that male dog to do his thing. He was beside himself over the job at hand, when Simone and I couldn't take it anymore and burst into hysterical laughter back on his front step. Marching back inside he informed us that our joke was indeed on him.

MISTAKES

This book would not be complete without telling you about my mistakes. I have made mistakes where the poor dogs had to pay the piper.

Cocoa had seven beautiful Cockapoo puppies. They all were pre-sold to hopefully loving homes, long before they were little more than squeaking bundles of fur. By five weeks of age, I knew I was going to have a problem with the largest girl puppy. By five weeks old, she was not advancing in the human-dog relationship at all.

She was so shy that every time I bent down to ruffle their fur or change their blanket or anything, she cried out in anguish. She literally crunched herself in a corner, presenting her belly in fear. This was not good. The family who had chosen her had three small, dynamite, go, go, go children. They needed a puppy who loved attention, not this quaking bundle of fear. By six weeks, she had gotten worse instead of better, as I spent a great deal of time just trying to cuddle and stroke her. I had no choice but to phone the people up and refund their money. I know that a lot of dog breeders would have just handed them this puppy at six (much too young) or seven to eight weeks old and never worried about it. I knew better. She was not the puppy for them.

I decided that I would just keep her and work with her myself. I named her Julie and then I screwed up. I started out with good intentions, but somewhere between the sixteen-hour days, the horses and the rest of the pack, I failed miserably in spending enough gentle time with her. She matured quickly into a fairly large-sized, athletic dog. She also became incredibly wild. So wild, that to catch her to groom her, worm her or give her shots, I had to corner her and trap her. Julie knows her name and always cocks her head when I say her name and talk to her. But no touching. She will even come to me and standing on her hind legs, for a split second place her front paws on my leg, but clearly says "don't touch me." Had I taken the time to give her away to a good, older, mature person while still a pup, I believe my Julie dog could have had a better life. Now she will have to remain here forever, a dog who will never know the joy of a belly rub, of falling asleep on her master's knee owing to a lack of time on my part. I should have known better.

Fleecy was another mistake. She carries terrible scars from when the pack tore her to shreds. She survived, I sometimes think, no thanks to me. I call myself an animal lover and I allowed this fury to happen. After coming to live with me, she urinated continually in the house. I made the decision she would have to be an outside dog. I introduced her to the first outside pen with moderate results. The five dogs in the pen tended to dominate her and make her life miserable. She was the second female dog I owned who has a certain smell about her that makes the other females want to attack her, to chew her to shreds. I brought her back into the house. I worked on her peeing on the floor, wishing she would learn to simply zip through the dog door and do it outside. I reasoned that it was because she came to a new home as an adult. Torn from her family (never messed in the house and never bit people) she now had bit two of my friends in the back of the leg. She topped it off by pooping on my pillow on two occasions when I left the bedroom door open. I was frustrated—she was even more so. She was not happy here. So I advertised her as an adult dog for adoption, free to a good home. Lots of people phoned. I had to honestly say that she was not properly housetrained in my home and that she had nipped visitors. Nobody wanted her.

I believe all Fleecy was trying to tell me, was that being sold to me, a total stranger, was too much for her to handle. I didn't listen. I spent several afternoons introducing her to the five dogs in the largest outside pen. They did not treat her well, but seemed to accept her without bullying her. Out she went. As I rotated them back into the house every few weeks, I hoped that she would learn to do her duties outside before coming back in for a time.

Fleecy tried to tell me that the situation was not good. She sat apart from the others, her eyes pleading with me. I didn't listen. Each pen has a camper-type dog house, heated to the same temperature as my house. Things were about to become deadly.

The male fox who was fond of torturing that particular pen of dogs by sitting outside their wire fence and mocking them was back. The snow was not too deep, so the hunting of mice was keeping him fat and happy. He came in the middle of the night and got the dogs screaming and howling and fighting mad by sitting inches away, grinning at them.

I didn't get much sleep. And I had a long trip planned for the next day. I jammed my head under the pillow and hoped to drown the savage snarling out as the alarm clock was set for five-thirty a.m. I almost hated that fox even though I admired his audacity.

Now awake I embarked upon my dog chores. Margo showed up bright and early to help with the horses. I was on my way out of town and had a long drive ahead of me with little sleep. Margo would accompany me, to help keep me awake through the long day ahead and to help drive back.

We were actually seconds away from leaving. The truck was warmed up in the frigid winter air.

Those five dogs had started up again with hurricane animosity. My brain finally kicked into overdrive. It was ten a.m. That fox was long gone. Even before full sunrise, he would have gone. They were after Fleecy! Rushing around for a clear glimpse of their heated home, I saw nothing but dogs frantically digging under their home. Frozen dirt was flying everywhere.

Then she appeared. The others clinging to her, savagely trying to bring her down. She made a life-saving dash towards us.

Margo, quick on her feet, was up and over that five-foot wire fence. She grabbed Fleecy and threw her over the top to me.

We carried her into the living room. No dogs in here, just two humans and one snow-white Bichon-Cocker. Except she wasn't snow-white. Matted with black mud, frozen ice, but very little blood, she clung to me. Please, oh please, don't put me down! I placed her on the couch and examined her. The small amounts of blood seemed mainly to be from her ears and some on her lips. When the others were trying to dig her out, she had sustained bites to her face. They were not serious, and trying to examine the rest of her body, I could not get by the build-up of mud and ice on her fur. She appeared to be, on further examination, in the beginning stages of severe shock. Life-threatening shock.

Stupid, stupid me. Irresponsible me. A dog in shock, may stop bleeding or show no outward signs of severe injury, but when they go into shock, the blood rushes to their internal organs. But I placed her in a comfortable kennel with food and water, told her that the crust of ice on her would soon melt and dry, and headed out of town.

Many hours later, we returned. Late at night. Margo first helped me with the other dog and horse chores. Then I went to Fleecy.

In a heated house all that time and still she was ice cold. She was also almost comatose. Practically no signs of life. I rushed her to the vet.

Upon shaving her naked, the truth of her injuries emerged. One whole flank torn wide open. Her intestines held in by only a thin membrane. Her neck, on the top side, ripped down almost to the spinal column. But she lived, no thanks to me.

And now she lives in the house. I cannot even trust the housedogs not to attack and attempt to savage her. The other dogs absolutely hate her. She now comes everywhere in the truck with me and Bailey. We have become close friends, her and I.

Why they hate her, the very smell of her, I do not know. But I do know that I could have spared Fleecy from enduring such pain. I was a fool.

DR. CORY

Dr. Neil Cory has always been there for me. After midnight, before the sun even thinks about rising, he is there. I cannot even begin to count the times I have awoken this man to come to my rescue for the caesareans, the seriously wounded horse or dog or the milk-fevered female dog on her last legs. He is always there, tired, worn out, perhaps wishing he had never even heard my name.

As I became a regular to his country clinic, I slowly became a part of his existence, someone who was always sitting on his doorstep, with another horse- or dog-related problem. The other local vets are great but have more regular office hours and my animals seem to prefer late-night disasters. In time, Dr. Cory was no longer just my vet but a good friend.

Dr. Cory has found more than one good home for the lost and unwanted. Such as the starving three- to four-month-old pup he found out in his cattle pasture. It was terrified of humans. Using a sandwich for bait he managed to convince the pup to come to him, one small bite at a time. Named Skyler, the dog now lives with one of Dr. Cory's past employees. After rescuing a lost dog out in the bush, he cleaned it up, removing its mattes and burrs, gave it the necessary shots and finally found the man it belonged to so it could go home again. More than one cat remains on the farm, finding a welcome place to live with caring people.

I have ended up at his family's kitchen table more often than not. I realize the love of all creatures that this man has through his experiences and stories. I would like to share with you some of the stories of his life with dogs as they were told to me.

H.B.A.

We vets often use abbreviations when referring to injured animals. If the patient was a human involved in a car accident, a likely abbreviation would be on the file, M.V.A. (Motor Vehicle Accident). With animals it would be H.B.C. (Hit By Car). The patient may be a B.B.D. (Bit By Dog), or the animal may be S.O.B. (Short On Breath). Zeke, the Black Lab, had to be different. He was H.B.A. (Hit By Aircraft).

Zeke had a peculiar habit—he chased airplanes. He also had a problem—he caught one.

Zeke belonged to a farmer and pilot named Jake. Jake not only flew his own plane regularly, he had several other farmers and trappers who kept their light aircraft at his private landing strip on his land. Now Zeke didn't chase cars like most dogs. He revelled in chasing those airplanes down the runway full out until they cleared the ground and disappeared into the heavens.

One spring day, Jake and his buddies taxied down the runway and prepared for takeoff. A day of fishing was in the making. Jake had no way of knowing that during takeoff, the dog would finally catch the plane. Or, shall we say, the plane caught him.

As it turned out, they would not be returning that same day as planned. As they were taking off to come home, the plane hit some flood ice and bogged down. Well, when you can't fly, you walk. Off they trudged to get some help. For the next two days, they used skidoos to pack down an emergency runway.

Meanwhile, Jake's dad went to the farm to check things out. There he finds the seriously injured dog. Zeke was some happy to see Grampa.

Amazingly enough, although when the dog was brought to me his leg was just dangling there, no arteries or nerves had been severed. After a five-hour surgery, three hundred stitches and two drains left in the wound, that black fool was up and going great guns. I kept him at the clinic for three weeks, while the savage wound drained and healed. Finally, I was able to remove the drains and resuture the remaining holes. Zeke walked out of the clinic a new dog.

That wasn't Zeke's last encounter at the clinic, although his second stay was for a very different reason. About three years later, he had decided to amble on down the road to town and do some visiting. The dogcatcher soon nabbed him and delivered him to the pound at the clinic. It was a week before my secretary realized that the Black Labrador Retriever lying quietly in the kennel was no other than Zeke. Speaking his name brought the big clown of a dog alive with happiness. He was saved again. He was soon back home with his master, Jake. And busy chasing aircraft again.

CATTLE BUYERS AND CATTLE DOGS

Cattle buyers are a rather distinct group of individuals. They tend to know all the country folk, their cattle and horses and their dogs for a hundred miles around their place.

When a cattle buyer named Al showed up at my place in the fall of '97, the first thing he said to me was, "Where did you get that black dog?" I replied that it had shown up at my place over a week ago and insisted on sleeping in my old farm truck used for fencing. The dog seemed to like people but really liked that old truck box better. Al said he bet he knew who owned that black Border Collie-type dog. Sure enough, the next day, one very happy horse trainer, named Francis, showed up to collect his cowdog. Now for the rest of the story.

Francis was a well-known horse trainer and a top stockman. Many times he would be called upon to come help different ranchers gather their cattle. He always arrived with a good horse and his black dog, Toby. Toby virtually lived in the back of Francis' truck and went everywhere with him. Seems they had spent a hard week at the Wolf Lake grazing reserve, helping jimmy those half-spooked cows out of the bush and trees. Toby working hard right along with the men.

On the way home Francis had stopped for lunch. He left town, not realizing that Toby had jumped out of the back of his truck to relieve himself. Once home, he realized that Toby was missing and not wanting to lose such a top cattle dog, backtracked to find him. No such luck. When a countryman loses a top horse or dog, it is a story that gets told and retold at all the auction marts in the countryside. Within a week, everyone was on the lookout for a lost black dog.

As for Toby, he wasn't much for being a town dog, and headed in the general direction of home. My pasture was on his route homewards. There, my two boys had been fixing fence. Toby, tired out from his journey, simply figured my old truck would have to do in lieu of his master's. So home he came to my place.

With the word out about him being missing, it hadn't taken Al, the cattle buyer, long to put two and two together and figure out where Toby really belonged. Now Francis double checks each time he stops somewhere to make sure that Toby is still snoozing in the back of his four-wheeled doghouse.

A DEADLY NECKLACE
Cold Lake Retrievers are an indigenous group of dogs that were developed in the Cold Lake Region during the

thirties and forties, quite by accident. Originally, most of the dogs were sled dogs used by the native trappers and traders to haul furs and fish from Primrose Lake and other areas to the railhead south of Cold Lake. Then during the thirties and forties, Labrador Retrievers were introduced into the country to help with duck and goose hunting. Dogs will be dogs and soon there was a growing population of sled dog and Retriever crosses. These crossbreeds turned out to be exceptional hunters. They were agile and quick to retrieve anything, even musk-rats. Many trappers and hunters found them perfect for bringing in the season's bounty of muskrats. To this very day, we still see a large number of the aptly named Cold Lake Retrievers. They are usually black with some white or yellow dogs. Most have a very thick tail and retain their quickness and agility. Back in the early seventies, a woman named Eva lived on the west side of the lake and still raised some of these dogs. She had no trouble finding homes for her well fed and cared-for pups.

Late one fall, one of her five-year-old bitches, named Chico, went missing. Chico loved to hunt in the woods on her own and Eva and her daughter-in-law, Lesley, searched every evening through the woods and along the roadways. She asked everyone she met if they had seen her Chico dog but to no avail.

Then very early one Sunday morning, Lesley went outside. In the quiet stillness of the crisp morning air, she heard a faint howl. Following the sound, she jour-neyed deep into the woods. There sat Chico, next to a poplar tree. Lesley called to the dog, but she refused to budge an inch. Coming up to the dog, she saw she was very thin and in poor shape, not at all like her usual plump self. She was soon to discover why the dog had not come when called and why she was so emaciated.

Chico was held firm around her neck, by a deadly wire rabbit snare. These snares normally kill their prey quickly. As the victim struggles, the thin wire noose draws tighter with each movement until the prey is choked to death.

Lesley quickly freed the dog from the tree and rushed her to me, with the wire still around her neck. Poor Chico had the wire deeply embedded in her neck. Thankfully no muscles had been destroyed and I was able to remove it.

The reason Chico survived the snare was because, having been tied to a tree at home before, she knew better than to struggle and choke to death. She had had enough fat reserves on her body to nourish her along with the bit of frost that would have gathered within her reach each night to lick for moisture. It must have been torture for her each evening hearing Eva and Lesley calling and calling her name and not being able to come to their calls. For the rest of her life, she had a ring of white hair around her throat where the deadly necklace had held her captive.

MIDNIGHT RIDE

Max was my dog and at his best when working with me. Typical of a lot of Border Collie dogs, he wanted only one master.

The cattle buyer, Al, was the first to point out the dog's devotion to me one morning when he came for coffee. He knew, before I could tell him, that I had been away from the farm the last few days. How he knew was simple. When I was gone, Max always waited for me in the driveway, just off the road. Seeing the dog there, Al knew it was no use to stop in for coffee because I wouldn't be there. My vet clinic is located now in my yard across from the house. Al said, if Max wasn't there in the driveway, then I must be home. So in he would come. If Max was at the clinic, he knew then that I was busy over there. If the black-and-white dog was on the house steps, then I was there and the coffee was on.

When feeding my cattle in their pens, my hired man, Paul, always had to get off the tractor and close the gate so the critters wouldn't get out. When I fed the cattle it was much easier because Max guarded the gateways and saved me the job of closing them.

Max loved to help move cattle through the chute for doctoring them. One pure-bred Charolais cow just hated that dog and would either try to kick the daylights out of him or charge him with deadly intent every time he came near her. Max bided his time, waiting for a chance to get even. Finally his chance came. This cow was in the chute and refused to move forward, just being ornery as per usual. I told Max to get after her and get her moving. His time had come. Darting in, he sank his teeth in her rear leg, by going after her under the bottom rail. Well, it worked and the cow shot forward. Except Max's fangs were caught in her leg and he couldn't let go. Luckily his lower canine tooth broke and he was freed of his predicament. He seemed a little more careful how hard he bit after that even if he didn't like the cow in question.

Late one night, a man brought in a cow for me to do a caesarean on. Max curled up in the cold snow near the door to wait for me. When I finally finished the operation, the Black Angus cow was quickly reloaded in the stock trailer, while the new-born calf was put in the cab of the truck beside the man for the long ride home.

He said he had a lot of trouble on the way home with the cow keeping that trailer swaying and swerving all over the road. He was soon to find out why. Once home, he opened the trailer door to let the cow out and out shot Max, with the irate cow hot on his tail. Obviously, during the operation back at my place, Max had figured curling up in the deep warm straw inside the trailer was a lot more comfy than laying in the snow to wait for me.

It must have been quite a ride all right: a black-and-white dog trapped with a mad black cow, inside a dark trailer on a moonless night's journey.

When I made the forty-mile trip to get him, I didn't even have the truck door fully open when he leapt through it and was up on the seat next to me. He never budged an inch all the way home to safety.

FOR THE LOVE OF DOGS

For those thinking about getting into raising dogs, along with the good times and the joy brought by these faithful companions, comes the bad times. The real bad times.

In one week, your faith can be shattered, almost beyond repair. Polly's pregnancy had hardly put a dint in her hunting skills. True, by August, the mice were getting few and far between and Polly was getting hard up to bring me her daily quota of special gifts. She was forced to resort to old bones and even a red sock that had mysteriously gone missing a couple of months before.

The first four puppies popped into this world, squeaking and squalling and hungry as baby wolves. Then nothing. Straining and panting, Polly just couldn't have that next puppy. Late at night as it was, she and I made the long drive to Dr. Cory. Pacing the waiting room, I prayed for my little girl to hold on through the caesarean operation as Dr. Cory worked at delivering the next puppies. He was unable to save the puppy that was so enormous that it simply couldn't be born on its own, but three other tiny wonders were given life because of the operation.

Back home, Polly shook off the last of the fog and settled down to being the tremendous mom that she was. The sun was already up by the time I made my way to bed for a couple of hour's rest.

My pets saw to it that I was up within what seemed like a blink of an eye; after all, they wanted their morning run and feeding. Even though they have a doggie door and total freedom out here in the country, they can't head out without me. Even though they have dry dog food in front of them, twenty-four hours a day, they have to have their special soft food right on schedule every morning and evening.

Polly appeared fine, but it was obvious that the puppies were not getting enough milk. Immediately I mixed new-born formula for them and started to feed them. One could not suck, nor swallow. Soon, he was gone. By night-time, another was gone. By the following morning, still another. Polly now had a raging fever. She was rapidly going down-hill and producing no milk at all. Rushing her to the closest vet, I watched as he hooked her up to intravenous. I headed back home to care for the three surviving babies.

My fat, waddling Peanut was ready to give birth. Again, problems. Another caesarean. No puppies survived, which was heart breaking for not only me but also the vet who tried so hard.

Tari Tari. My precious Tari Tari. I had decided to allow her to have a litter of pups. Stupid of me, stupid. Tari gave birth to a single, snow-white pup. She laid happy and proud with her pup in her basket placed beside my pillow on my bed.

I guess I had always known that Tari's heart was not strong. As she had huge swollen dugs, milk galore, I gave her Polly's babies too. Now she was even more proud. A true mother finally.

For a week, she proudly cared for her own baby and Polly's surviving three. She radiated happiness as only Tari could.

Three or four times per day, I came in from my outside chores, opened the bedroom door and asked her if she was ready to go to the bathroom. "Oh yes, please," she seemed to say. You see, Tari would not get up on or down off the bed without me lifting her. That was simply Tari's way.

That day was a bad day from square one. Out in the corrals, the local vet fought to get food and water down a sick horse. The horse took up almost the whole day. As soon as he left, I headed for the house, after all, Tari couldn't hold on forever without a bathroom break. Opening the bedroom door, I asked her how things were going and if she wanted me to lift her down so she could make a beeline outside to the bathroom.

My girl was so happy to see me. Possibly she thought I was never coming for her. One second she was bouncing with excitement, grinning with happiness over me remembering she was there, the next second, she was dying. You see, her heart gave out. She had a severe heart attack. She died in my arms. It was over within seconds. She was gone.

Stunned beyond belief, I held her still warm body and told myself, no more, I can't take it anymore. I quit. No more. Let the puppy mills raise puppies in their cages. Let the puppy mills, who don't care for the adult dogs' comfort and happiness, raise puppies. I quit. Let the other horse people raise the horses, let me out of this life. Then those four puppies started to squirm in Tari's basket. They were looking for her warmth, her milk, her gentle tongue to clean them.

Tomorrow, I could cry the blues. Right now, today, those babies needed me. Polly was back on her feet, healing nicely. But she had dried up. Although she was still sad over the loss of not being able to be a mother, she was going to be all right. She could be spayed in a few weeks and just be happy being my number one provider of odds and ends for the rest of her life.

I would just have to raise the pups on formula. And that's where my Peanut dog comes back into the picture. After her operation and the loss of her own litter, Peanut had been laying around healing up and getting well. She had not been in full milk at the time of her loss. Now she showed me yet again that my pack of friends have something special going on in their world.

I was busy mixing formula at the kitchen sink, listening to those hungry babies in the bedroom, crying and making a fuss. I wasn't the only one listening. Peanut was sitting in front of the closed door, whining and snuffling in worry over the babies' noises. When I entered the bedroom to feed them, I saw no harm in allowing Peanut to come in with me, as she was really starting to be bothered by the babies' cries. Peanut, who was built too low to the ground and too pudgy to jump up on the bed, made it up on the bed on the first leap. In a flash, she was in Tari's basket with those babies. Nuzzling them, licking them, she curled around them and raised her lip at me to let me know that as the mother of these pups, she meant to protect them from me if I made the wrong move.

Within eight hours, she had come into her milk just like she had just now given birth. For Tari's baby, she was her second mom. For Polly's little ones, she was their third mom, all in one week.

My dogs never cease to amaze me. They show their intelligence, their love and their caring in so many unique ways.

That particular week was devastating to me. But four innocent new-borns survived to carry on. Tari Tari will always be with me. Her memory will stay bright and fresh in my heart forever. Stay close to God, my Tari Tari, you deserve everlasting happiness.

TO SAY GOODBYE

They come to me as rescued dogs or from ads in the papers. They come to me and I find a place in my heart for each and every one of them. Yes, they produce puppies for me if they can. Yes, I make a profit off those puppies if they are healthy, of good temperament and sellable.

They give me, not only profit, but unconditional love, as only a dog can. They are never far from me, never far from my heart.

But I can't keep them all forever. So decisions have to be made. The ones who can go on and become members of an ordinary household, do. I don't give them to just anybody. I try, sometimes for months, to find the perfect home for them. Every one phones for a free dog or a cheap dog. I screen those callers, like I said, sometimes for months. People sign an adoption agreement that the dog will be spayed or neutered. If they and the dog are not compatible, then they can return it to me. My little ones are not throw-aways.

As for my friends, such as Tika, Scruffy and Betsy—had I known, had I been able to see that I was putting your very existence and sanity at risk, believe me, my friends, I would not have done so. I'm so sorry. Please forgive me.

Lady, Domino, Pebbles, Pongo, Sophie, Snoopy, Cinnamin, Cash, Sarah Lee, Tee Tee, Peanut, Taffy, Colleen, Julie, Angel (no. 1), Angel (no. 2), Dagwood, Odie, Sammy and several more all found good homes. Special dogs like Brat and Ralph found even more terrific homes. It took two years to find Kirby a home but Pat and Harry love her. These dogs and more now have the homes they so desperately needed. The love even I couldn't give them. Thank you people.

My furry friends who are not placeable, who are not able to comprehend a new home with new rules, remain with me. They grow old knowing that I love them. They are my children.

The Author

Gayle Bunney was born in the town of Oyen, in south-eastern Alberta. Her parents, Ralph and Rebecca Caskey still live there, although they are long retired from the farm where Gayle grew up. A longtime lover of all animals and birds, she is especially fond of her horses and dogs. She not only raises an array of different breeds of dogs, she also takes the time and expense to rescue as many unwanted dogs and other creatures as possible. She knows she cannot save them all but says to save even one dog from a life of despair makes her life worth living. Now residing in Bonnyville, Alberta, she loves to joke that she has gone to the dogs. Perhaps she has!

Her first book, *Horse Stories, Riding With the Wind*, was published by Lone Pine in 1998.